Deeper Than a River

Adventures of a Wandering Fisherman

Teryl "T" Johansson

DEEPER THAN A RIVER

ADVENTURES OF A WANDERING FISHERMAN

www.bearcreekpress.com/teryl.html

PHOTOGRAPHS BY
Grant Burkman, Dale Franz, Tim Hall,
Teryl Johansson, Brian O'Keefe, Mike Oxman

ARTWORK BY
Mim Lagoe of Lewiston, Idaho
Teryl Johansson of Enterprise, Oregon

PUBLISHED BY
Bear Creek Press
814 Couch Avenue • Wallowa, Oregon 97885
541-886-9020 • bearcreekpress@eoni.com
www.bearcreekpress.com

PRINTING HISTORY
Versions of some chapters have appeared as articles in such magazines as *Trout*, *Flyfishing*, *The Flyfisher*, and *Salmon Trout Steelheader* from 1984 through 1989.

Bear Creek Press First Edition, June 2004

FRONT & BACK COVER PHOTOGRAPHS BY
Brian O'Keefe of Powell Butte, Oregon
www.brian@brianokeefephotos.com

Printed in the United States of America.

ISBN: 1-930111-42-8

World Headquarters located in Wallowa, Oregon U.S.A.
(at the old Abbie Riggle place on Bear Creek Road).

Dedicated to My Four Dads

Grant Burkman, beloved father,
The one who led me to the river.

"Fast Eddie" Suttner, fly fishing mentor,
The one who kept my boots wet.

Don Keefer, wordsmith & wisdom-keeper,
The one who always believed in my storytelling.

The Creator,
The One who made me an Artemis Woman,
kin to all things wild and free.

Contents

- Introduction 7
- Summer of Silver 9
- Fast Eddie 17
- Silver Talons, Sacred Prey 23
- *G-G-G-Girl* Fishing 27
- Pisces Rising 33
- A Madison Vignette 37
- Number One (First Steelhead) 39
- The Gift Fish 45
- Baked Alaska 47
- A Long-Legged Lesson 53
- The Royal Guilt Fly 57
- The Deli Special 61
- Guadalupe-River-Bottom-Pudding-Pie 67
- Worming My Way 73
- The Magic Caddis 81
- Redside Rodeo 85
- Professor Brown 89
- The Bear Essentials 95
  - Part I: Russian Roulette 96
  - Part II: The Real Katmai Fisherman 99

Poems

- Mom's Not Here 26
- Silver Reflection 32
- Heaven 60
- The River Church 66
- Off Season 80
- It Takes a River 108

Introduction

Here's to the river,
the wondrous creatures dwelling therein,
and those who wade among them.

If my Dad gave me one gift more precious than any other, it was my very first fishing rod and time alone with him on the river.

A thousand sacred memories are wrapped inside the laughter and silence we shared during all those years we were fishing buddies. My father's fishing deeper waters now, exploring new pools and secret eddies, preparing to teach me those, too, I suppose, once I'm old enough *again* to join him.

The author's father teaching her to wade

In the meantime, I'll settle for the warm smiles of remembrance—for old stories and new stories yet to be written, like every fisherman does. In some mysterious way we never quite fathom, each cast retrieves yet another small but essential piece of ourselves, adds one more subtle line to the shape of who we are becoming, fills in just enough color and texture to make a life worth remembering.

Ask any *real* fisherman—it was never really about the fish.

Jeryl T Johansson

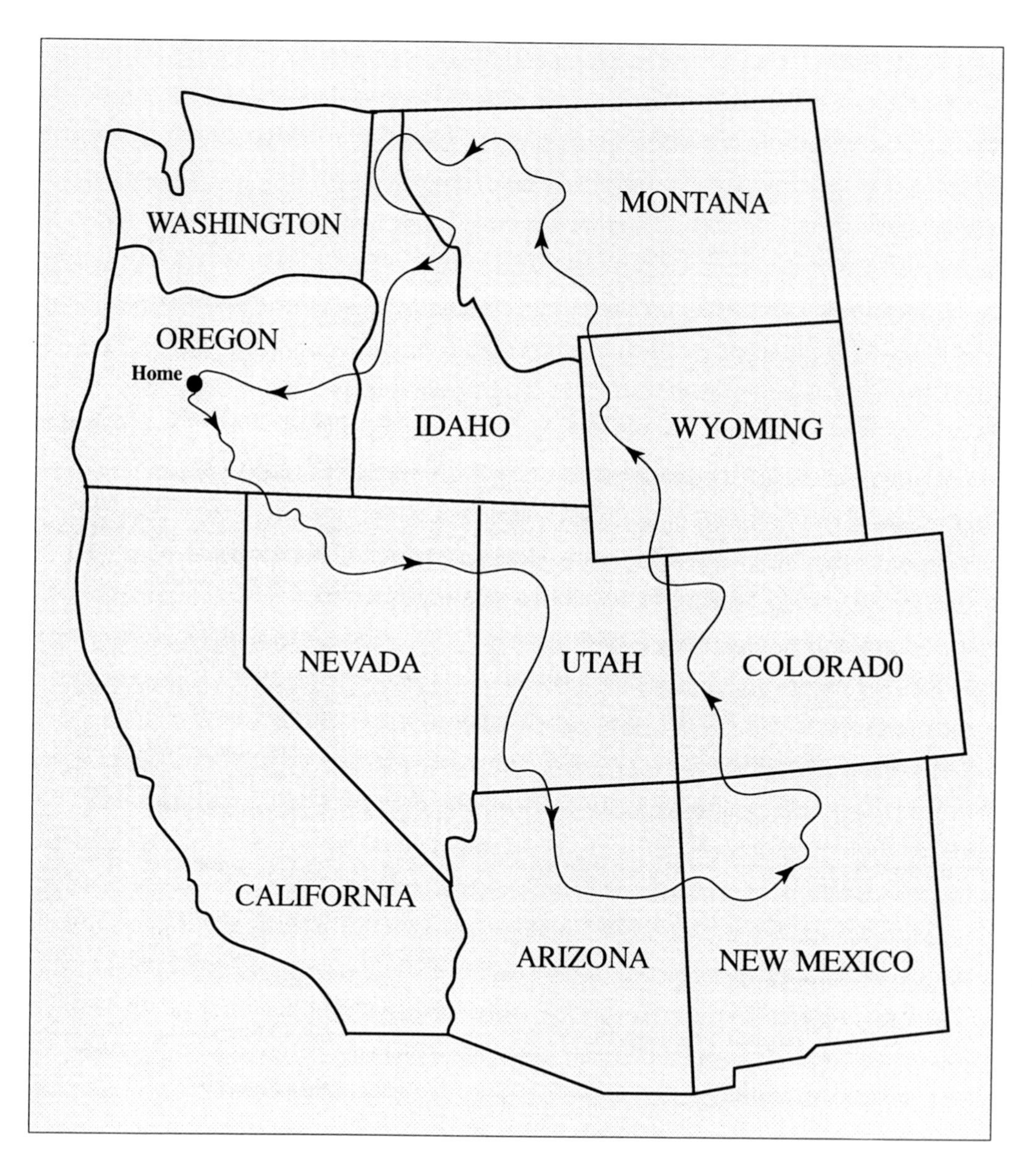

Summer of Silver
1984

Summer of Silver

Friday, June 15, 1984. Noon. One of those cloudless central Oregon days. The engine idled as I slid the last rod case into the slender compartment at the side of the van. Unfished, I pulled it out for one last look—my first custom-built graphite 9-foot 3-inch, 6-weight, arriving just yesterday by express mail from my pen pal in Helena, Montana. I rolled it reverently in my hand. The twenty-inch marker, the special inscription, "Ms. T," gave it magic. A wizard's wand. And we had a fantasy to catch!

Friends had paced and muttered all spring, their gloomy forecasts kept pouring in. Roadside peril! Watery doom! A woman traveling by herself was just asking for it, they warned. So I'd made two concessions: to camp only in established campgrounds and, in wild water, to wear a carbon dioxide cartridge vest. Period. Beyond that, I was determined to give this lifetime gift to myself—a summer alone on the famous trout streams of the West. Was I crazy? Probably. And about to have the time of my life!

Fishing the Southwest would be spotty at best, but one major objective still drew me that way. It wasn't long before I'd seen enough dry creek beds to create a great thirst, and I raced for this ace in the hole.

My excitement was boiling over into another medley of, "Oh, give me a home where the wild cutthroat roam" as the VW chattered down the last half-mile of washboard toward New Mexico's famed San Juan River. Finally, the massive spillways of Navajo Dam loomed high above me, just as the dog-eared article in my lap promised. This had to be the catch and release stretch that held the trophy trout.

I'd given my winter over to reading every book, magazine, and personal chronicle I could lay my hands on in preparation for this trip. As my boots slogged through the swampy backwaters, not even the hordes of biting, blood-sucking insects could penetrate the trance.

"Light Hendrickson emergers, size 18, dead-drifted near the bottom." That was the word at the gas station several miles downstream. It had been a long and difficult approach, and I was sweating heavily as I broke through the shoulder-high grass at the river's edge.

Ten a.m., late for desert country. Enormous shapes scuttled from the dense weed beds that choked the shallows near the bank. Half a dozen well-spaced anglers worked the huge channel at the far side. I moved to join them. At mid-thigh the deceptive river gave a powerful nudge, sent me skating along the treacherous bottom for several yards before I regained my footing. Far enough. Someone had drowned here yesterday. I quartered my 6-weight sink-tip and waited for the bump. It wouldn't be long now. Some people are born with the gift of finding fish—I'm one of the lucky ones.

Two hours, forty pounds of "seaweed" later, I was still waiting. With every cast the line came back looking like a multi-colored flag banner at your neighborhood used car lot. The fly was invariably buried in a fist-sized wad of green glop, and I was about to give it up when a sympathetic local spied this damsel in distress and waded up beside me.

"See you haven't learned the San Juan Slap yet," he said, demonstrating with two bull-whipping casts, allowing the third one to "grenade" onto the water. "First two will clear your line. Next one's for real. Doesn't spook 'em, they're used to it." And he was gone.

Pays to be a woman sometimes. Chivalry was not dead, at least on the San Juan. I counted two nice rainbow that day and one good lesson in humility. But I still had a lot to learn.

Teryl on Montana's Missouri River

Feeling more at home the farther north I moved, I worked my way into the mountains of Colorado, wading any pond, puddle, or rivulet that looked inviting. Fly selection by guess and by golly became the order of the day. A few standard patterns produced steadily—the Adams, Hare's Ear, and my personal favorite, a size 12 gold-bodied Bucktail Caddis. But when all else failed, the little roadside cafe became a dependable reference library where, if you chose the right stool next to the right old-timer, somewhere along the course of a cup of coffee he noticed your waders and struck up a conversation that went something like this:

"Fishin'?"
"Yep."
"Where from?"
"Oregon."
"By yerself?"
"Yep."
"You kiddin'?"
"Nope."
"Any luck?"
"Some...but I can't quite figure it out."

Suddenly it's like E. F. Hutton is talking. Place has gone quiet as a church. Folks are leaning way over in their chairs, listening. Another joins up at the counter and that's when the fun begins.

Any fisherman worth his salt knows how to spin a good yarn, and it isn't long before the whole joint is poppin' with each self-proclaimed expert outdoing the other, dredging up secret formulas faster than I can take my mental notes.

I'm wondering now, from this vantage point, if a woman traveling solo like this doesn't have a distinct advantage over her male counterparts. Perhaps she's perceived as less of a threat. A novelty. Who cares? It's one heck of an entertaining way to learn the local scoop. Throughout my nine-state adventure, wonderful folks drew maps, called ahead to friends, swapped meals and flies, and fished side by side with me. It was an unforgettable, heart-warming experience.

I was chest-deep in Soda Lake, six miles outside Pinedale, Wyoming, when the first bolt of lightning struck five hundred yards behind me. Normally I display a healthy respect for Nature's temper, would have cut the fish loose and "beat cleats" to the car. But the scrappy two-pounder was stripping my Hardy for the third time, and I didn't have the heart. I decided to take my chances.

(There's a letter to my son in the bottom of my underwear drawer. It reminds him that I died doing what I most loved to do. It's been waiting there for more than thirty years—just in case.)

Anyway, I knew the icebox was empty, so I'd already planned to make a rare exception and invite this fish to dinner. Rumor had it that Soda was the official brood lake for all the brookie and brown trout in Wyoming. This guy was a guppy compared to the grand-daddies reputed to inhabit this water.

In a few minutes I was lighting the votive candle, gorging myself on mushrooms and wild rice, sautéed brown trout with fresh lemon, and a tall paper cup of Riesling. Decadence. You have to give in to it once in a while.

I stretched out in the back of my metallic cocoon to enjoy the remainder of the storm. Encased in an echo chamber of howling wind, pelting rain, cracking thunder, and Dan Fogelberg tunes, the last thought I remember—life is good.

Daylight broke with a harsh reality. I stared at my last mangled Stovepipe, regretting now that I'd opted to leave the bulky tying kit back in Oregon. Well, I'd just have to pick some up tomorrow.

But each region has its favorite flies, and the old Oregon standby hadn't even hit the charts in these Rocky Mountain states. Green chenille body, weighted. Orange and black pheasant-tippet tail. Mallard feather laid flat over the back. Everywhere I looked the story was the same: "Stovepipe, you say? No. Sorry, never heard of it."

I fished my way through Yellowstone without it. By Livingston I couldn't stand it any longer. This fly had been taking fish! I made my deal with the proprietor of a little side-street tackle shop. For the price of the materials and a copy of the pattern he'd give me a few minutes at his backroom vise. Sold! Thus the coveted pattern made its dubious debut in Montana, and I walked away re-armed with half a dozen of my beloved fish-grabbers. But the real test was yet to come.

Montana. Mecca. To a fly fisherman it means the same thing. This was it. The dissertation. The final exam. July 24th, Helena. I rang Bill Dunham's doorbell, anxious to finally meet this man at the far end of my postage stamp.

Bill was the director of the Montana Land Reliance, a very effective non-profit conservation effort dedicated to the preservation of the state's agricultural land and scenic waterways. Our mutual fanaticism for fly fishing had given rise to four months of spirited correspondence.

Now we stood face to face. The friendship was instantaneous. He was a warm and gracious host, opening his home to me as a headquarters for the next month while I spun off to explore the wealth of western Montana's magnificent fisheries.

"Sorry, T', but I have to be in the office tomorrow. Why don't you try your luck on the Prickly Pear?" He penciled out directions, commenting that if I went far enough I'd run smack into the Missouri, just below Holter Dam, where the really *big* fish were.

Big fish. That erased everything Bill had said prior to that—and next morning I drove straight to the banks of the Mighty Mo'. Big fish and plenty of them. The river was virtually boiling. Trico hatch. I was so clumsy with excitement it took fifteen minutes to gear up! Bill's parting words, "Keep a couple for dinner," kept ringing in my ears. With all this bounty, what could a couple hurt?

Photograph by Grant Burkman (Teryl's dad)

The author fishing Idaho's Silver Creek during her Summer of Silver

I fished hard for nine hours. We had fish for dinner all right—*tuna.* Dunham's cautious remark, "Smart, aren't they?" was meant to smooth it over, but it came out "skunked" no matter how you looked at it, and my new friend rushed to revive my expiring ego.

We launched his canoe about nine o'clock the next morning in approximately the same stretch I had stalked so ineffectively the day before. Under his astute guidance, my second cast yielded the prettiest sixteen-inch brown you've ever seen! Took a size 18 black-and-white trico spinner, *twitched.* File that one away.

I fired a streamside voice tape back to my fishing buddies in Oregon. "Twenty-five beauties in one short afternoon!" I burbled. These burly trout were snapping 4X tippet like sewing thread, devouring size 10 Joe's Hoppers like so much popcorn at a Saturday matinee!

"Fast Eddie" swooned. At nearly seventy years of age, my dear friend and piscatorial mentor wanted nothing more than to join us in Montana. This incredible man fords Oregon's swollen winter Deschutes with all the grace and agility of the great blue heron, extracting (and releasing) countless numbers of twenty-inch-plus trout from the frigid river with amazing regularity. How I got lucky enough to team up with a master of this caliber—well, that's another story.

The Madison, Gallatin, Fire Hole, Big Hole, Missouri, Rock Creek, Henry's Fork—I fished them all. A fishing rod is like a magnet to those of similar persuasion, and up north in Glacier Park I met a delightful couple just completing a record-breaking 27,000-mile bicycle tour of the United States. They had spotted my waders drying on the line and wondered if I'd mind giving them a lesson. We hooked a twenty-pound beaver in little St. Mary's River that night, the stuff memories are made of.

And so each night I came to write a new page in an old diary, curled up in the back of my trusty camper, somewhere along 9,000 miles of western

America's trout country. With the ragged map yet draped across the dash, I rest eyes that spent their days scanning for the rise. And while echoes of some angler's tale still bump inside my brain, I'm off to where imaginary hooks are set to jerk me wide awake again! I wait. I plan. And if you ask me why, the honest answer isn't *fish*—or I'd be standing at the seafood counter with everyone else, saving myself the trouble.

No. I'll have to say it's more to do with catching my own reflection in the early morning glass. With finding time to feel and test. And some unspoken passion.

Every soul yearns for clear expression. For me it comes together when I'm wading a riffle, flicking a fly. Then everything fits. I know it looks a lot like "fishing," but sometimes I wonder if this isn't just the excuse I use to go down and stand in a river.

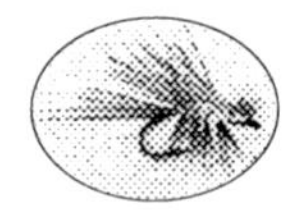

Fast Eddie

Portrait of a Mentor

I cradled the belly of the hefty brown a few seconds longer than I needed to—there is an indefinable emotion that accompanies the releasing of a beautiful fish. It is a very private moment. I watched as one sweep of the powerful tail returned him to the emerald shadows beneath the ledge, swallowed hard and turned.

Only then did I remember where I was and who had brought me to this magical place. Eddie's eyes beamed down on me from the path above. Eddie *understood.*

Hours went by without a word, but plenty passed between us on that river. Eddie had a way of drawing my attention to the subtle rise, of pointing out the fragile mayfly dancing through the air. A nod. A glance. A certain furrow in the brow. He was a master of the obscure. He taught and I listened. Tonight I got an *A*.

Not many nights before, another fishing companion had pulled me from my half-eaten supper with an excited, "Hey! There's somebody you've gotta meet!"

That somebody turned out to be a barrel-chested, ruddy-cheeked, white-haired gentleman set on devouring an enormous slice of lemon meringue pie—a somebody filled with quips and quotes and river jargon, an instantaneous friend.

It suddenly registered that I was meeting the legendary "Fast Eddie," central Oregon's maestro of the dry fly—right there in front of me, eating pie! And before I knew it he was saying, "Caddis are on, when do we leave?"

And I was stammering, "Er...Monday, right after work?"

And he was agreeing, "Fine!"

And, *My Gawd*, I was going fishing with the master! And that's how it all began.

Well, somewhere around four o'clock I started expecting the phone to ring at the office where I worked as a dental hygienist.

"Hello, Dr. Urda's office," the receptionist answered. "Yes, but she's with a patient right now...5:30? I'll tell her." I knew who it was and what it meant—Bingo!—we were goin' fishin'!

The author and Fast Eddie

I kept my rod handy for occasions just like this, flossed that last mouth with new-found vigor, threw on my blue jeans, and headed straight for Ed's. We'd pitch his gear in the back and be on the road in less than ninety seconds. Carl Edward Suttner. They didn't call him "Fast Eddie" for nothin'!

Sometimes I'd make him a batch of homemade granola as an extra special "thank you." Sometimes he'd slip me a copy of his latest wildlife sketch. It was becoming a regular mutual admiration society, only we held our meetings on the river.

"Have you heard the latest? Fast Eddie's trying to teach a *girl* how to fly fish!" The town was all abuzz. He was stretching some old-time friendships mighty thin, crossing the gender barriers like this. But somehow Eddie always made me feel like I was worth the trouble.

So whenever we encountered another "What's-a-woman-doing-on-my-river" look, Eddie just figured we still had a little educating to do.

With a fifteen-second assessment of current, rise and hatch, his reassuring wink would launch me into position just down-riffle from our latest Doubting Thomas. Then as I set to work extracting fish after lovely fish from under a disbelieving nose, Eddie danced his internal victory jig.

Lost in the frenzy of yielding trout, it might be an hour or more before I'd look up to find Eddie and our Thomas sharing a nearby stump. "She comes up a little short on that back-cast, don't ya' think? There, you see?—a little hitch in there. We'll have to get rid of that." And the three of us would fish out the night together.

We were chalking-up an impressive number of hours on the river. By now I had learned to handle the tricky currents, the fly-eating foliage, even the demanding roll casts with reasonable dispatch. But today I was facing an invisible foe that no one had warned me about. Frustration, thy name is *wind*.

As one rejected cast after another piled up in an outrage of garbled line, I was succumbing to the easy despondency of a rank beginner. Eddie poked his head through the willows. "What d'ya say we take a break?"

We sat down on an old gray log, shoulders touching—my stifled tears still begging for release. Eddie gazed overhead as the big pines twisted. God love him, he knew I felt beaten.

"Do you know what I do with a wind like this, Teryl?" I waited for the pearl of piscatorial wisdom that was sure to follow. "It's quite simple. I just fold up my tent and go home."

My tension disintegrated into a gale of uproarious laughter, and we strolled arm-in-arm to the car.

An aborted fishing trip can set the mood for philosophy. Today I would be wading the heart of my mentor. "Don't let it get you down," he counseled. "There's an awful lot to learn. Heck, I pick up new tricks every day. That's what keeps me coming back, I'll never know it all." I felt immensely better as that one thought took residence in my mind.

"You gotta remember," he continued, "I've had some kind of fishing stick in my hands for over sixty years. You get to be a pretty fair judge of who's *got it* and who doesn't in that length of time. I can teach some folks to throw a decent fly in a matter of hours. Some it takes days, weeks. Others quit. But you're the first woman I ever started that stuck with it. Don't you worry, you're one of the *naturals.* You're comin' along just fine." That was the kind of encouragement he always offered—the reason Eddie had trouble counting up all his friends.

"Strangers stop by to watch you fish. So you give 'em a couple of flies to try, or a casting tip, or a lesson on reading the water. I get a big kick out of watching somebody hook their first fish on a fly. I remember this one guy—almost *wet* his own waders he got so excited!" He chuckled to himself, obviously reliving the joy-filled event.

So this is what makes an expert fisherman turn mentor. This is what gives him the fortitude to tolerate a water-thrashing greenhorn. Pieces of the puzzle were starting to fit. Eddie was so filled with his passion for fly fishing that it simply spilled over wherever he went. He'd drive the newcomers right down to the fly shop, advise them on the prices and relative merits of the gear. Then he'd fish alongside them until they got it right. "Shoot, who knows? They might work into a good fishin' buddy someday. You can never have too many of those."

"The biggest mistake most beginners make is trying to throw too much line too soon, before they get the timing down. Besides that, on a lot of streams like the Metolius here, they're throwin' right over the top of the fish." Eddie's on a roll.

"Lots of fish, right at your feet. *Nice* fish. Like the one I put you on last week down at Lower Bridge." He referred to a spunky seventeen-inch Deschutes brown trout he'd given me position to catch. "I've caught so many of those big guys, why'd I want to catch another one? But you should have seen the look on your face!" The look on my face—the look that was worth a king's ransom to Eddie.

"No siree, you get all those young bucks out there tryin' to muscle that fly a hundred miles—they're missin' the boat. Finesse and placement. Observation and patience. That's the name of *this* game." He followed the same theory on the golf course, and he beat 'em to the clubhouse every time.

He became reverent for a few minutes then, talked of tradition and a sport with a proud heritage—one without much of a future if we didn't all pitch in to save it. He talked of conservation, of barbless hooks and catch and release programs, of the decades of drastic change he'd witnessed with his own eyes. Fast Eddie: The Ambassador for Fish.

Part jester, part sage—he drifted off into another anecdote I'd heard a half-dozen times but would gladly hear once more. Ed and his old crony had come down to their favorite fishing hole late one evening to find it crowded with holiday anglers. The friend was already beating a disappointed retreat when Eddie came up with a bright idea, as Eddie often does.

"Come over here, Sid, and don't ask any questions." Donning an adoring countenance, Eddie took Sid by the hand and promenaded his mortified companion up and down the riverbank. "Why, we had that whole darned pool to ourselves in a matter of minutes," he flashed with an incorrigible grin. Oh Eddie—you *didn't*. But I know for a fact that he did.

Or what about the time Eddie met the disheartened fisherman returning from the Metolius River's *Dolly Hole*. "Broke off a monster," he confided to Ed, showing him a duplicate of the fly that had almost done the trick. "Tried for an hour, couldn't raise him again."

Eddie knew the fish. Knew its habits. Knew its lie. And he had just the fly that could do it. So he took his time getting down to the river, resting the fish another twenty minutes before he stepped up to deliver the deadly cast.

Landing like the proverbial butterfly on sore feet, the fly settled perfectly in the feeding lane. Eddie braced for the strike. Nothing. Second pass. Nothing. A third time and—*Whaammm!*—two warriors strained at a gossamer thread.

A young couple picnicking nearby drew closer to watch. Sensing a gallery, Eddie began a blow-by-blow commentary for the mesmerized pair. He remarked in intricate detail on the great trout's size, species, and gender, adding casually, "Watch now, when I land her—there'll be my fly, and then this little redheaded peacock pattern stuck way over in the *left* corner of her jaw."

It was only a fifty-fifty chance, but plenty good odds for a showman like Ed. And sure enough, as he gentled the fish each of his predictions came true.

The baffled couple wandered away, shaking their heads. It seemed that the uncanny demonstration had proven a little too much for them. Eddie sighed inconsolably. "Shoot!" he grumbled, kicking at the dust. "They got away without the clincher. I was just about fixin' to doff my hat and walk off across the water."

Now, most of us enjoy the help of a mentor somewhere along the way. He is the father, the uncle, the old family friend—anyone who finds the time to take the "kid" in us a-fishin'. But when he also manages to cast a magic spell over the entire fishing experience, to fashion in us a certain reverence for the solitude, for the rivers, and for the magnificent creatures dwelling therein—well then, we have met our own "Fast Eddie."

He sets the heart-hook strong and deep. And occasionally walks on water.

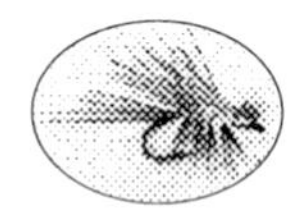

Silver Talons, Sacred Prey

A Story of Initiation

In The Beginning, there was no light. But there was a fishing rod. And a tiny, leaky rowboat. And a young girl who wasn't afraid of the dark. I was only seven and it was better then. I hadn't been taught what was possible yet so I believed in *impossible* things.

At this moment I am just a little girl, in a tiny rowboat, in the middle of a great big lake, and *I am the only human in the world.*

So many days begin like this one—tip-toeing barefoot across the cold cabin floor, easing the screen door open so creaking hinges won't disturb my slumbering parents. I slip the required life jacket over my arm, fumble in pre-dawn shadows for the icy handle of a rusty old tackle box, once more trust the shiny silver tip of my very own fishing pole to show me the way.

Steam rises from the glassy surface of the lake as dawn gathers on the eastern rim. My young soul fills with fresh wet forest smells, the familiar crunch of dry pine needles underfoot. I grow taller with each step. I am The Lonely Huntress, coming.

With one quick push, the bow of my worthy eight-foot pram cuts the liquid mirror in two, and soon the steady cadence of bumping, dipping oars calms my pounding heart to a mesmerizing pace. The sweetest music ever played, this soft squeaking of the old oars' rotted leather wrappings called once again to patient service. I lean and pull, lean and pull, summoning all my fledgling strength. Mists part, invite me into a different world now, one where seven-year-olds are full of power.

I've made one full pass along the rocky shoreline, point to point, as far as I'm permitted to go. A stern old-country father has clearly defined my boundaries. If I row beyond sight of the cabin, I'll lose my boating privileges for a long, long time. It isn't a risk I'm willing to take.

Mim Lagoe

I'm fishing shallow this morning, as the kokanee always cruise the surface at this time of day, picking off the early morning hatches. My single fluorescent lure wiggles and flashes some thirty yards behind the boat as I make a wide slow arc, circling back for another pass. Suddenly, an ominous feeling jolts every cell of my being. I glance up just as a huge silent shadow moves menacingly from behind me, quickly obliterating the sky only a few feet above my head. It is *so* BIG and I am *so* small. I instinctively hunch down and close my eyes tight, bracing for the sharp talons that will surely stab deep into the back of my neck, carry me away.

Instead the huge bald eagle swoops low over the stern just inches above the water. In one deft and impossible movement, it stretches massive wings and claws to pluck a squirming fish from the exploding surface, then evaporates silently to the north. Fear retreats with the great bird as a new realization slowly begins to form inside my swirling mind. "Oh…he's just a fisherman…like *me*."

The eagle and I are inexorably connected from this moment forward. We are creatures with common path and purpose. We understand each other. On some level, we are kin.

I am left breathless, trembling, electrified, completely adrift in an ocean of awe, marked by an encounter so profound, so utterly unexpected, so foreign to any previous experience that I'm forced to carve a new opening in my child's reality. My vision of the world and my place in it has suddenly stretched light years beyond former limits. Unharmed, but far from unchanged, I will draw strength and insight from this threshold moment for the remainder of my life.

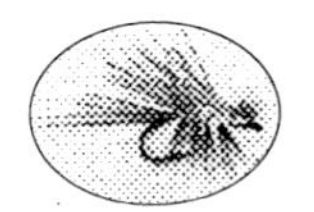

Mom's Not Here

You'll have to call back sometime after dark,
she's down to the River fishin' again —
'least her rod and her vest
are gone off the peg,
and that's where she goes
when the day's been too long.

She told me once,
but I don't understand
how a River will *talk* if you're quiet enough,
how sometimes there's trout
and sometimes there's more,
but always there's somethin'
for takin' the time.

Says she finds peace
when she gentles a fish,
turning it back for the River to keep,
takes all the answers the River will give,
giving thanks that a River can *speak.*

G-G-G-Girl Fishing

"You're bringin' *who*?" That's how it usually starts. Then comes the eye-rolling, some mighty hard looks, and a lot of not-very-comfortable silence. I generally take a magazine to read while the boys work things out.

I'm not exactly a *girl* anymore, but there was a time when I walked that path, and it was often beside a trout stream. This doesn't seem to count for much with some of the good ol' boys who still think any place holding water and fish (including all territory within a fifty-mile radius) is a man's exclusive, sacred domain.

It happens precisely because I've been blessed with a number of very gutsy fishing buddies who've come to consider me "one of the guys," but that's generally taken some time. This is the part they forget when offhandedly inviting me along on another outing with chums I haven't met. Guys being guys, advance notice is out of the question. Me climbing out of the truck is usually the first heads-up, followed instantly by the first thumbs-down.

I once took these snubs rather personally, but it soon became a sport of its own. I really do "get" this classic knee-jerk reaction, sort of. If I figured *I* was going to spend a fair share of my day unsnarling a city girl's fishing line, or listening to her squeal if she takes a surprise dunking, or even gets lucky enough, God forbid, to actually hook a fish, I might not be too keen on the whole idea myself. But hey, I'm no radical feminist out to eradicate men's poker night—I'm just a gal who loves to go fishing.

I remember this one September day down on the Deschutes River when some lifelong friendships got stretched to the max.

The fella who laid his life on the line that day was signed up to haul all five of us and *The Wee Sourdough*, a pretty little honey-colored wooden driftboat with more fishing experience than all of us combined. I was first on the pick-up list. The other three would be waiting (impatiently) at Fast Eddie's place a couple of miles away.

Sure enough, when we pulled up they were all standing around a pile of gear in the middle of the condos' parking lot, chomping at the bit. I watched as a couple of casual glances radically transformed into a riveting glare. Good thing my window was half-way down, or I might have missed the start of the fireworks.

As we jockeyed the trailer around, the young man with his back to us now was hissing through his teeth, "Oxman brought a G__ d__ *broad* with him!"

Yikes! I was about to spend a couple of hours packed like a sardine in a can with these guys—might be a pretty tight ride.

My buddy knew I'd overheard the jab. "C'mon, T," he said, "let's go kick their ass!" As I recall, by evening that's pretty much what we'd done.

Now, these three were some high-powered, serious fishermen. Fast Eddie, of course, had been my primary fly fishing mentor for years, much like a second dad. Even though Ed was pushing well into his 70s, not many could out-fish him. He was the stuff legends are made of, and we were cool. But these other two hotshots—Mark and Danny, squirtin' Copenhagen spittle and struttin' around like a couple of wet-combed banty roosters—they still had some proving to do. Looked like I was all lined up to be the lucky recipient of some serious attitude.

I sat up front between Ox and Eddie. Mark and Danny gladly claimed the backseat, as far away from the *broad* as possible. We didn't hear much from them all the way to the river—likely they were way too busy staring holes into the back of my head.

The author as cover girl

It took a little over an hour to drive from Bend to the Madras store, where we picked up our special day permits for fishing the "Indian side" of the river. We'd be cooped up another forty-five minutes or so, making our way toward Culver and the Gateway cut-off. That's where the pavement ends in a bumpy, dusty descent into the well-known stretch called Trout Creek. Here the Deschutes skirts the Warm Springs Indian Reservation for a number of miles, a section notorious for holding some of the biggest rainbow "redsides" in the river.

Things remained palpably tense as we stowed our gear and launched the boat. Today we'd only be using *The Wee Sourdough* to ferry us across to the other side. From there we'd do the rest on foot, working the banks and wading the wide, swift riffles to our hearts' content. It's big water there—slick, cold, and fast with plenty of tricky currents, deep channels, and holes. A person had to be careful, but at least there was plenty of room to avoid the *broad.*

The sky already carried the cobalt tinge of early autumn, and a gold and crimson promise hung in the streamside foliage as our worthy craft slid past. I always feel very quiet, very reverent and respectful heading into a place I've never been. Suddenly, our boat bumped ashore and the adventure began.

This was my first experience with Trout Creek, and it was going to take a while to get my bearings. I'm tall enough but lightweight, so it's plenty easy to get blown off my feet. Even with a good wading staff, the huge, algae-coated boulders made wading extremely precarious. My cleats helped, but not a lot.

Everyone else quickly dispersed to their favorite spots. I stumbled around and finally found a decent foothold in about two feet of water near the edge of an okay riffle, as deep as I wanted to venture in such powerful current. I was glad to be wearing snug-fitting neoprene chest-waders with a tight wading belt in case I went down.

Obviously too late for the morning hatch, I switched to a sink-tip line, tied on a good old standby wet, a well-weighted gold-ribbed Hare's Ear, and gave it to the stream. The reward was almost instant—a brilliant, scrappy little redside hen, not quite fourteen inches long—an absolutely gorgeous fish, fat and feisty, just the way I like 'em. Combined with this heavy current, even a modest-sized trout made for a memorable fight. Man, oh man, this was going to be great!

Releasing this first fish, I suddenly had that odd feeling of being watched, looked up just in time to catch the quick flash from mirrored sunglasses on one of the roosters downstream. It made me chuckle. I've never minded a bit of healthy competition and can usually hold my own.

Well, I could see we had ourselves the makings of a fishing derby here, and I decided to sign up. "I'll see your Hare's Ear, and I'll raise you a Wooly Bugger, you little bugger!" It kinda went like that.

We were diagonal in the river—I was shallow, he was deep—with a good hundred yards and a broad sweeping corner dividing us, but we never missed a move. Sometimes the rooster pulled ahead by a nose, maybe two, then I'd come in with a bigger fish. Then I'd have the numbers and he'd have the size. Things might go dead a while, and we'd both start rooting around in our fly boxes, frantically searching for just the ticket to break things loose again.

All morning I matched that rooster fish for fish. I *knew* I was having a ball and suspected he was feeling pretty much the same.

The sun was sliding well down in the sky before I started thinking about lunch. I just hated to give that cocky rooster any unfair advantage, but I had to have something to eat. All our food was stored in the cooler back at the boat, so that's where I was headed when a deep, booming voice spun me around.

"Hey!" The two roosters were walking up the path behind me, but only one of them spoke: "Lady, you can *fish*."

I grinned, they grinned, and that was that.

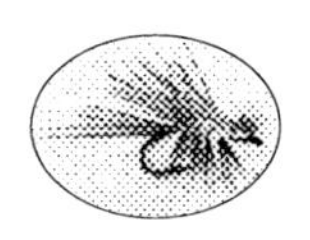

Silver Reflection

When I cast to you
I'm really casting to myself,
to the wildness that still lives deep in me,
and to instincts I've almost forgotten.

I was wild once—like you.
I gathered my food and clung to my life
with the same ferocity.
I was sleek, and lean, and proud,
like you.

Now, sometimes it takes a hook
for me to test and trust myself again,
it takes your strength
to remind me of my own,
and I'm sorry if it causes you much pain
for I never meant to harm you.

Pisces Rising

The Slow, Sure Hatching of a Fly Fisher

Before the age of 32, the closest I ever came to a fly was swatting one on the wall. I guess we'd trailed a few behind a bobber at one time or another, but I seriously doubt that counts.

When I fished with my dad, though, especially in later years when we almost exclusively trolled Oregon's Crescent Lake, our gear invariably included a long string of gaudy silver flashers. With so much tugging action of their own, unless you hooked a whale it was hard to tell the difference between a real hit and the monotonous pulsing drag of the two ton hardware.

Nope, back in the '50s and '60s we were bait fishermen, spin casters, and trollers, and plenty proud of it. Worms, salmon eggs, lures, and the occasional flat-fish—that's what I knew something about. When I was alone in my trusty little beat-up rowboat, *Lightning,* I sometimes fished these pure—just the line, a leader, and whatever was wrapped around the hook. I liked the simplicity of that. It seemed to suit me much better somehow, long before I understood why.

One lazy August morning I was out early, just drifting around. As usual, the heavy cool air was coaxing woodsmoke down from the long line of cabins, piling it up in thin, curling wisps over the surface of the lake. I was down toward the lower end, watching someone I didn't recognize chop kindling on top of a broad flat stump. It always amazed me to see the axe fall a full second or two before the sharp *thwack!* of the splitting wood would reach me way out there on the water.

Lightning drifted closer and closer to shore as I hung over the side, daydreaming and staring down into the lake. Then I spotted something white and round resting near a shadowy ledge. We were always finding broken-off tackle on the rocky bottom and had the entertaining habit of trying to retrieve it if we could. Once in a while it turned out to be a worthwhile effort, but most of the gear was ruined and ended up in the trash.

The author working on her boat, *Lightning*

This was different from anything I'd seen before, so I rowed to shore and scrambled up the loose pumice banks to the pump house where we stored the glass-bottom box Dad had built for occasions just like this. Made of wood and painted bright orange with a flat black interior, the big box was clumsy to use but improved underwater viewing by two hundred percent. I scrounged around for an oversized treble hook, grabbed my fishing rod and the box, and wrestled it all back down to the boat.

It took a few minutes to relocate the strange white disk in more than twelve feet of water. Through the viewing box it looked like some kind of tackle container. A loop or strap hung off one side—that's what I'd try for.

I tied on the big treble hook, pinched on a heavy split-shot right above the eye, and lowered my makeshift grapple into the water. It was very hard to hold the rod with one hand and balance the bobbing box with the other, but once I finally pinned both rod and box against the stern of the boat I was in business.

After a bazillion passes with that hook, the mystery disc was finally on its way to the surface. Whether it was valuable or not, I felt pretty proud of myself. And when the mysterious object was finally in my hands, what a treasure!

It was one of those flat, round, plastic tackle containers with the pie shaped compartments—you know, the ones with one flip-lid you rotate until you reach the section you want. The container itself was cool enough, maybe a little worse for its underwater adventure, but when I opened it up—Wow! It was chock full of fishing flies, soggy but still intact, in shapes and sizes and colors I'd never seen before. Pure magic.

Well, I cleaned and dried each of those flies carefully, one by one, and kept them in that same little box for years, like a shrine. And I wondered about them and about the person who lost them. On quiet nights by the cabin fire, I'd take them out, sort through them again, line them up like a platoon of little imaginary soldiers. But I never used them. I didn't know how.

Guess that box got lost over the years, though I'm not sure how. I just know that's when the fly fishing seed first got planted. It wouldn't sprout for another twenty years, but when it finally got watered by the right set of circumstances, it shot up like a magic beanstalk overnight. I've been climbing it ever since.

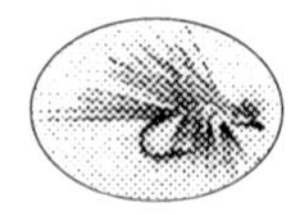

A Madison Vignette

There's no hint of delicacy in the first savage strike—the massive rainbow simply smashes the Hopper and brings it down in a singular, explosive arc. I am too startled to set the hook; the big silver hen sets herself with her own ferocity. She turns for her station between the rock and the high grassy undercut before either of us registers an impediment. With one shake of her head, she cuts wildly for the dark, heavy current beyond the calmer trough, but the flex of the rod and the 3X tippet cause her to settle instead on a somber sulk twenty yards below, and far outside me. Now, at least, I have a chance.

Wading Montana's Madison River: "It's like dancing on greased bowling balls," according to anyone who's ever done it. That truth suddenly rises like some perfect emerger to the surface of my mind. An icy, warning trickle makes it over my wader-tops, signaling the end of a most awkward and arduous advance. It is fully ten minutes before my trembling hands are retrieving the tattered remnants of a number eight Joe's Hopper from the wondrously broad, green snout. I whisper my thanks to four pounds of well spent fury before she slips back into her river.

No other matches her size or strength on this sultry, thunderheaded afternoon, but many rival her ferocity. They feed in ravenous abandon, devastating every fat olive-gold terrestrial that falls, flutters, or purposefully launches itself onto the sacrificial mirror along the river's edge. Shifting to a lighter tippet, I break off more than I mean to, but I am lost in the reckless frenzy of a timeless, ageless cycle. Prey and predator. Both or neither, it doesn't matter. It only matters that I am here, and somehow a part of it.

Reaching blindly for another Hopper, with a frazzled tippet dangling from my teeth, my fingers suddenly transmit the harshest of realities: the box is empty. There's not a single Hopper left! I toss a Muddler, then giant Drakes and Jugheads, but still the quiet slick remains. I measure a potential road race to the gas 'n tackle shop many miles upriver against the angle of a quick-sinking sun, but am forced to decide against it. In utter desperation, I attempt to manifest the tying kit lying uselessly on my workbench back in Oregon, nine hundred miles away.

I sit motionless in the pale, parched grass as teasing naturals adorn my arms and hair. Eyes closed, I absorb the sloshing song of cycles quite unfinished, all the while constructing a solemn promise to myself. Next year, I will be here, pockets bulging with Moonglow Hoppers, sizes 6 and 8 and 10. In early August. Mark my words. When the 'hoppers come, I will be here.

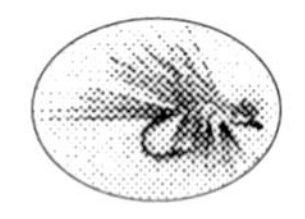

Number One

(First Steelhead)

The doctor's ultimatum—"Absolutely no casting with that arm"—makes it halfway through my brain. My head nods in seeming acquiescence, but my heart is whispering, "We'll see."

Frozen shoulder, he calls it. At ten percent mobility, there was a lot of deep aching, too much medication, and a sling. But that was over a month ago. Things are moving a lot better by now, and I'm not likely to turn down another rare chance at taking my first winter steelhead.

There is a slow, sick, grating sound and a rush of whirling tires as the truck half backs, half skids down the icy loading ramp. I squint my eyes against a vision of boat, trailer, and truck, complete with driver sinking quietly into the dark, frigid depths of the early morning Clackamas River.

"Worse than usual," is Frank Amato's unruffled comment as he hops from the cab to tend the drifting craft. As it turns out, this is just the first of many thrills in store for me today.

The engine starts without a hitch, and in an instant our jet boat planes smartly upriver at speeds that utterly astound me. I've always been a summertime, rowboat gal, you see. "Bring plenty of warm clothes" makes more sense to me now as I zip the parka hood up over the back of my neck and tuck my hands tighter between my knees.

The shoulder isn't bothering me now—what's a frozen shoulder when you have a frozen nose, frozen fingers, and frozen legs to boot? I settle back, growing accustomed to the cutting harshness. So this is winter steelheading, huh? I'm waiting for the rain—or snow—to make the day complete.

"Let's try this run first," Frank suggests. "We'll see if we can pick up an easy fish."

An "easy fish," I learn, is any steelhead that can be hooked within the first hour or two of fishing. Frank hands me a standard rod and reel outfitted with some iridescent aberration that looks like an over-sized ponytail bobble attached to two enormous, freshly-sharpened treble hooks.

"B-b-but, Frank," I protest weakly, "I'm a *fly fisher.*"

His eyes betray his amusement. "Not if you want a fish, my dear. Not today you're not."

The gaudy gold plug is swallowed almost immediately by the emerald green currents, and old childhood recollections begin to stir with the tug-tug-tugging rhythm of the foreign rod pulsing steadily in my hands.

"Hey," I blurt, "Dad and I used to fish with rigs like this when we trolled the lake for kokanee." Maybe this plug thing's going to be all right.

Steelhead. Enigma to end all enigmas it seems. Wish I had a nickel—no, make that a dime—for every theory that contradicts every other theory surrounding this mysterious, elusive creature. It eats. It doesn't eat. It defends. No, it attacks. It survives the spawn, it doesn't. It prefers water between fifty-five and fifty-seven degrees. Not so. It strikes best at forty-eight. But the air must be warmer than the water, and the river must be falling, and the barometric pressure rising, and the prevailing winds must be coming from the southwest, with Jupiter conjuncting Mars on the third Tuesday after the first rain in the months that begin with L. Even accomplished steelheaders will admit there's plenty of daylight between fish, and it's undoubtedly in these endless spans that such imaginative folklore gets invented.

And so it was, after carefully consulting with every authority known to man, I finally decided, what the heck. I'll fish with anyone who even *pretends* to know about steelheading, and maybe, after two or three hundred bone-chilling hours, I'll come up with some solid answers.

It is within this befuddled, half-hopeful resignation that I drift absent-mindedly down the wintery Clackamas with the endless tug-tug-tugging cadence of my rod nearly lulling me to sleep. I waver at the edge of semi-consciousness only by testing an occasional absconded steelheading theory against my patient captain.

"Sometimes, but not always," begins his answer to my query. Naturally, I figure, and catalog each ensuing response with all the others, somewhere under "Vague to Uncertain Habits of the Steelhead Trout."

I watch as another of the river's stoic sentinels, a great blue heron, settles gracefully into position on the smooth, round stones of the farther bank. The auxiliary engine purrs quietly, bucking the current just enough to allow our worthy vessel to drift oceanward at half the pace of the overly-anxious river beneath us.

Our rods bob mindlessly in their cylindrical holders while we rest our arms and alternately thaw our toes and fingers over the glowing grill of a tiny propane heater placed strategically between us. The canyon walls present an ever-changing mural of chocolate marbled with gold, and occasionally, when we escape the shadows, a weak January sun makes a pointless attempt to warm us.

Suddenly, I sense Frank shifting positions, and turn to see his hand resting lightly on my rod. "Fish—that's a fish!"

His lips form the long-awaited words around the stem of his still-smoldering pipe. I grab for the rod butt with the instincts of a long-time trout fisher, leaning back just a little to ensure penetration of the hook.

At this moment, the rod bends double and it registers, first in the incredible force exerted against my hands and then in the astounding impact finally transferring to my brain, that this is no eighteen-inch trout. This is A FISH! A REALLY BIG FISH! Nothing like this heart—this heart now pounding in my throat—has ever risen to before!

A million thoughts are sparking, ricocheting through my mind. "Geesuz! Did I set the hook hard enough? If I set it again, will it pull out? The knots. Oh, no! The knots—did I take four turns or five that time? Please, let them hold! WHOA!"

The line screams and the reel spins like a child's toy, surrendering to the weight of the runaway fish. Both fists jam the cork butt into my ribs, seeking more leverage on the rod. My shoulder aches, but it doesn't matter. Nothing matters. My senses are transfixed.

The action becomes a series of freeze-frame stills. I flash on the line as it enters the water, cutting a deep V in the shimmering surface as it tracks the diving fish. Now I see the huge dorsal, now the tail—look at the size of that tail! So far away, yet still as broad as my hand.

Swirling, slow motion, the curve of the massive back pushes a mountain of water first this way, then that. "Don't let this fish break off!" I implore the gods. "I'll do anything, *anything!*" My first steelhead! I can't believe it.

"She's a BIG one." Frank's voice enters from a world apart. "Might go fifteen pounds."

I *HAVE TO HAVE* THIS FISH! GEEZ, WHAT A FISH! And then the line goes slack. My heart sickens, slides from my throat to my knees. I am frozen, paralyzed, lost in the dread of what this means. I am unplugged. Flat. Blank. There is nothing on my screen. Suddenly, the light snaps on.

"No, no, silly! She's *charging* you! Reel the slack in—FAST!"

My mind jumps into overdrive, hands fly to meet the new command. A wonderful strain is coming back to the rod, and my heart is leaping with the fish. The water explodes and there she is, full length and twisting wildly, a living pillar of pewter and spray. She porpoises and dives, cutting widely from mid-river to shore, then sharply back again.

Can you love a fish? At this moment, I am certain that you can. She spots the boat and runs again, seeking the aid of the riffle far below, but she is tiring at last and finally turning.

I am dragging her now, a stone she seems, her every effort spent. Reluctant, I can feel her weary resignation in the rod, in me. I close my eyes. I almost have her.

Six feet from the boat, she turns half-heartedly, rolls, rights herself, then rolls again. This must be the moment when the picadors rush in. I'm sad. Well, almost sad.

"A net?" I ask.

"No, she's dark and full of eggs," Frank warns, "a net might be too hard on her."

So with a gentle hand he takes her by the tail and lifts her to my eager arms. My prize. My tarnished silver trophy, safe. I release a great sigh of relief.

A blur is all I'm seeing now—two corners of a mustached grin escaping around a camera lens, a squirming coppery mass too dense to lift, a stream of glistening, tangerine beads spilling down my trembling legs and out across the deck, a searing need to get this mother back into her river!

T's first steelhead

I never see her leave. My friend does this honor for me now and leaves me to myself. For a long, quiet moment I am caught somewhere between grief and celebration. I roll a tiny amber remembrance in my hand and hold it to the light. How can something so small contain the seed for such magnificence?

Tomorrow the canyon, the river, perhaps even the steelhead, once she has rested, will all be the same. But I…I will be different.

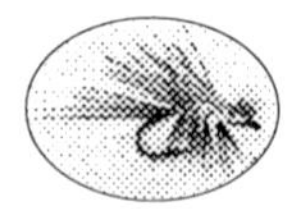

The Gift Fish

For me, in the very beginning, fishing was just another excuse for spending time with my dad. When he drove a forklift, I rode on his lap. When he drank buttermilk, I drank buttermilk. When he fished, I fished.

But everything changed on the day I landed my first little five-and-a-half inch rainbow—*without* his help. That's the moment I fell head-over-heels in love with the watery experience itself, with everything it would soon awaken in me—my independence, self-sufficiency, courage, curiosity, creativity; my fierce affection for all things wild, for the sweet poetry of silence. The person I am was born on that day.

We were just below Leaburg Dam on Oregon's McKenzie River. This wasn't a stretch of the river Dad usually favored, but today he was looking for some safe, shallow water where his almost four-year-old daughter could finally hook her own fish.

More than five decades later, I can still regenerate every volt of the powerful emotions that coursed through me as a tiny silver creature dangled from the end of my quivering pole. Shock, ecstasy, and pride soon faded into sadness and confusion when Dad said we'd have to kill this little fish if I wanted to show it to my mother. I closed my eyes and the terrible deed was done. (Years later I learned the fish's back had then been quickly snapped to gain the extra half-inch of stretch that might fool an unsympathetic game warden. I've never felt right about that.)

Before long, Dad and I were measuring our success by "the first, the biggest, and the most." With a buck paid for each triumph, we were always vying for a three-dollar-day. Whatever the outcome, I gleefully cleaned the entire catch to prove myself tough and worthy—slit open the soft white bellies, stripped out the guts, ran my little thumbnail up and down every spine till it sparkled. I carefully dissected at least one stomach each day to discover what they were eating, just the way I'd been shown.

The closing ritual for every outing was always the same. First our catch was carefully spread out across the front lawn, row after shimmering row. Then it was dutifully admired by the next door neighbors, who would gratefully haul some of it away. Soon Dad would crouch low, pull me onto his knee, and begin extolling the streamside prowess of his beaming young daughter. At last my non-fishing mother would emerge from the house, camera in hand, to capture yet another black and white snapshot for the already bursting family album. I always slept wonderfully, if a bit erratically, on those nights, repeatedly jerking myself awake with the setting of imaginary hooks.

No one really talked catch-and-release in those days; the resource seemed virtually inexhaustible—fish were meat for the table. Sadly, we often caught more than we could eat and a fair number of freezer-burned sacrifices eventually wound up at the city dump, victims of our short-sighted ignorance and an overly zealous spring cleaning.

We still had a lot to learn. Fortunately, the "gift fish" held out till we learned it.

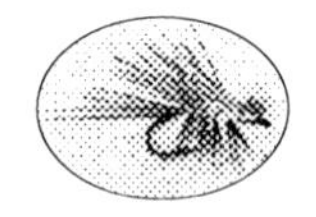

Baked Alaska

Among the wild and woolly legends of the rugged North Country, come the irrepressible tales of heroic scrimmages with man-sized fish, eagle-sized mosquitoes, leg-gnawing grizzlies, hundred-mile treks, eighty-pound packs, breakfasts of beans, and lunches of beans, and suppers of beans (if you can still face them), horizontal summer rains, rafts that leak, tents that leak more, and cold, soggy sleeping bags brought along mostly to soak up the difference.

Now don't get me wrong. There was a time in my life when I would have welcomed such rugged "elegance" as an essential ingredient for a true Alaskan adventure. Fortunately, I have survived my youthful misconceptions and arrived at the gates of sanity some call their "forties," when a soft, warm bed, a hot shower, and hot food rank right up there with oxygen and water as life-sustaining necessities.

In deference to those hardier (or fool-hardier) souls who here shout "Sacrilege!" from the wind-ravaged crags of their stoic bastions I retort, "Have at it, mate! Enjoy your beans! I'll take my Alaska *baked,* thank you—and lest you lose your taste for beans, for God's sake, don't read on!"

Many of us dream of fishing Alaska, quite aware that the pages of some wilderness magazine are probably as close as we'll ever get. So imagine my utter delight when at long last my dream came true, and a fairy tale journey sent me soaring perhaps a mile above the *real* Alaska!

Already the menacing drone of our engines had stampeded several moose through the thick underbrush and, only moments later, sent a magnificent grizzly on a defiant, lumbering retreat.

The pilot, undoubtedly entertained by a plane full of obvious first-timers, dipped the tiny cockpit earthward. My stomach took another not-too-crazy-about-flying mini-flip, as his finger extended toward my window.

"That's one of the rivers you'll be fishing," he explained. A twisted, silver ribbon uncurled in the dense tundra beneath us. "See that thick, dark shadow in the water?"

I regarded a nearly unbroken black band, clearly some kind of spring runoff silt, stretching fully one-third across the river's width and flowing like a river-within-a-river as far as I could see. "Yeah, what is it?' I asked politely, figuring I finally had one up on him, but not wanting to offend.

He searched my face, as I understand it now, for some hint of excitement, some flicker of recognition in the eyes. Clearly he'd overestimated me. "Those are *fish*, lady!" he rebounded. "That's what you came here for."

I laugh to imagine the way my head must have snapped back around to that window, how the amazing power of that split-second realization magically transmuted *silt* into *salmon,* and how every fishing story I'd ever heard about Alaska suddenly rang true.

Four seatbelts disengaged simultaneously as we all pressed our naive noses against the steaming, starboard glass. The rivers of Alaska really *do* run black with fish! The cockpit filled with an ever-escalating frenzy until a gentle deceleration and the soft swooshing of water finally brought our pontoons to rest. No doubt about it, these pilots were pros.

An even dozen we were, gathered for a mid-July week at the prestigious Alaska's Wilderness Lodge. The lodge is nestled on the shores of scenic Lake Clark at the northern head of the Alaskan Peninsula, 180 miles southwest of Anchorage, in the heart of the world-famous Bristol Bay watershed.

From the lodge we would have access to some of the finest fishing in the world. Three Cessna float planes, five Avon rafts, and eight riverboats would take us there. Every evening the guests would decide their next day's destinations—each plane could fly a different direction, stop at two or three locations along the way. We'd fish for kings, reds, silver, pink, or chum salmon; steelhead, rainbow, grayling, arctic char, northern pike, Dolly Varden, or lake trout—whatever our hearts desired.

Today we'd all decided to fish for "reds." (By the way, only "outsiders"—and we certainly didn't want to be known as one of *those*—call them *sockeye.)* Our planes landed on a tiny lake, and we fire-lined our gear ashore. We hiked a short distance across the tundra, to a bend in the river. Awaiting our arrival were two more guides as well as five Avon rafts packed with provisions and equipment. Soon we were drifting down the same silver ribbon we had so recently viewed from high above, dispersing the tight black band of sockeye spawners as we glided silently along.

A fresh surge of adrenalin invaded our veins each time the black shapes scuttled past us. A gentle breeze greeted our eager faces, a friendly overcast played hide-and-seek with a lukewarm sun.

Before long we were wading knee-deep and casting only ten or twelve feet into the shadowy mass. One reel screamed, and then another; or was it *me* screaming in sheer amazement as my back arched against the power of that first fish?

All I know is that suddenly I was hooked to a copper freight train, and it was bending my 8-weight almost double, moving unhindered toward deeper water, paying out the last of my backing incredibly fast!

When we could hold them, almost every cast yielded a six- to eight-pound beauty, ranging in hues from the brightest polished silver to the deepest, most tarnished brass. These were the glorious "reds," noted as much for their lithe, aerial acrobatics as for their long, powerful runs. My arms ached already, though my journey through Nirvana had scarcely begun.

As near as I could tell, these impressive fighters would strike at just about anything. Most of our party used spinning gear and became equally successful with a broad variety of lures and spoons. Being a fly fishing "purist," I stayed with large, bushy streamer flies, the gaudier the better I soon discovered—any color, predominantly silver-bodied, heavily weighted, and fished from a full-sinking or sink-tip line. (Next time, I think I'll wear a *helmet;* you can knock yourself out with those things!)

Teryl playing with the reds, Tanzamia River, Alaska

Some of the fish were foul-hooked, making their landing and release doubly difficult. Dorsal-hooked fish suffered little impediment and were able to maneuver "full powered" almost indefinitely. I attempted to palm my reel—but only once. (The burns are very slow-healing.) Side-snagged or tail-hooked reds weighed in at just shy of two tons apiece, while their fair-hooked brethren were only slightly less resistant. Give me a break, guys—I only weigh 110 pounds!

After three hours of ecstatic fishing, I collapsed into the bottom of our beached Avon, weakly delivering bits of broken chocolate to the corners of my slackened mouth. Before long I was able to sip nourishing liquids, and eventually sit almost upright—only to view my comrades having all that fun without me, and rise to the challenge once again. It was a dirty job, but someone had to do it.

We had worked up a powerful hunger when, as if by magic, a smoky aroma wafted out across the water from the nearby trees, where several guides motioned us ashore. There, like the proverbial feast in the wilderness, lay a gourmet extravaganza complete with grilled onions over freshly broiled sockeye fillets. We gorged and rested, rested and gorged, until it was time to sacrifice ourselves to the reds once more.

Emerging from the river's mouth at day's end, we were the weariest and most contented of travelers. A few die-hards made "one last cast" as our tireless guides readied the planes for departure.

Back at the main lodge, a full-course gourmet meal was being prepared for our evening enjoyment. Fresh trays of hors d'oeuvres waited for each of us in our individual cabins, sustenance as we saunaed or showered ourselves back to reality. Our last night's menu of prime rib and Yorkshire pudding, with all the trimmings, provided the main course. And for dessert? You guessed it: Baked Alaska!

I've turned lots of pages on the calendar since then. I've thawed out my last red fillet. But I can still feel Alaska under my boot-soles, see her black bands of salmon running up from the sea. Her glaciers still glisten off in the distance, and her wood-smoke still wafts through the trees. Perhaps no one ever really leaves Alaska. I doubt she'll ever leave me.

There must be myriad ways to experience Alaska. Some will choose to follow the "high road" like I did, while others still opt for their beans.

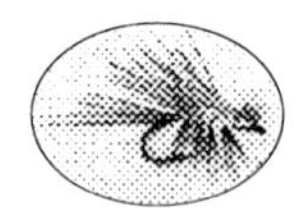

A Long-Legged Lesson

When you're born with the gift of finding fish, it's easy to get cocky. Obviously due for another too-big-for-your-britches lecture, I certainly got mine one day.

Now, I'm generally a catch-'n'-release kinda gal, but this particular morning I awakened with an irresistible hankering for fish flesh. Nothing too important showed up on the calendar, so I grabbed my trusty 5-weight and headed for the icy headwaters of Oregon's beautiful Metolius River, not six miles from my door. Heck, it wouldn't be any problem filling the frying pan by noon.

As it was, I thrashed that gorgeous water all day long to no avail. I tried every fly in the box, changed positions a hundred times, changed lines, never touched a fish. By late afternoon I was slumped against the trunk of a giant ponderosa, staring blankly downstream, licking my wounded pride. Suddenly a loud clatter directly cross-river jerked my head around.

I couldn't see what was causing all the commotion at first, but the uppermost branches of the tallest pine were swaying violently. Crash! Bang! Crack! The shuddering foliage complained unceasingly until a broad, slow-motion shadow finally drifted to the ground. There, still barely discernible against the dark, dense undergrowth, stood the largest, most majestic great blue heron these eyes had ever seen.

It was impossible to suppress an audible chuckle. How could anything look so regal and cool after, just seconds before, cartwheeling ass-end-over-tea-kettle down through the trees?

My amusement was short-lived as I fell under the powerful spell of this most intriguing piscatorial master. To this day, I've never witnessed a finer, more impeccable demonstration of inexhaustible patience and uncanny stealth, essential qualities for any masterful fisherman. Well, I sat straight up in my streamside seat, taking detailed mental notes:

Waits motionless in dark cover, 6-8 min. Stretches tall, slowly rotates head in imperceptible increments until 180-degree arc of river is meticulously scanned (approx. 5 min.) Reverses direction, repeats entire process twice again. Leans forward slightly, fixes gaze. Subtly bends left knee, slides left foot forward several inches, just microns off ground. Shifts weight onto advancing foot, duplicates nearly invisible movement with alternate legs until toes reach water's edge. Head drops slowly, heron continues silent, ghostly glide into stream till both knees submerged. Stops, still as stone (legs so thin, no wake observed).

I am un-breathing, unblinking, mesmerized as the glistening golden eye rolls briefly in its socket, clearly tracking some minuscule underwater movement invisible to me. Another full minute passes. Suddenly the water explodes and SHAZAAAM!—as if by magic, a hefty ten-inch rainbow squirms high above the river's surface, doomed by one lethal lightning jab.

I never once took my eyes off this Oscar-winning drama, yet somehow I'd missed the final act. I knew there was a bird without a fish. Then there

Mim Lagoe

Great Blue Heron

was a bird *with* a fish. I could only guess what happened in between. I'd witnessed a feathered Gary Cooper at high noon, but never saw him draw!

Surely I'd blown the final curtain call, but the show wasn't over quite yet. This long-legged a*fish*ionado still had some gloating to do. Just as the retreating heron reached the shallows, it turned to stare this empty-handed fisherperson squarely in the eye. Once again it raised the flopping silver trophy high, this time as if to say, "And that, little gal, is how it's done!"

Then—swear to Buddha, and I do not lie—that cocky bird began to strut its stuff up and down the riverbank before finally downing, in one rude and fluid gulp, the succulent supper that should have rightfully been mine.

Well, it wasn't the first time I'd been skunked, but it was certainly the first time I'd ever been skunked by a heron. Without further adieu, my dark nemesis unfurled great wings and lifted effortlessly into a fading sky.

Can't remember much about the drive home, except for a few mumbled, actually rather clever, disparaging remarks I might have cast toward that scrawny, pompous, needle-nosed, pencil-legged show-off somewhere along the way.

It took a while to adopt a more evolved philosophical perspective. Some days just don't turn out precisely the way we plan 'em. I got my fish dinner all right—if only another mammoth slice of Starkist humble pie.

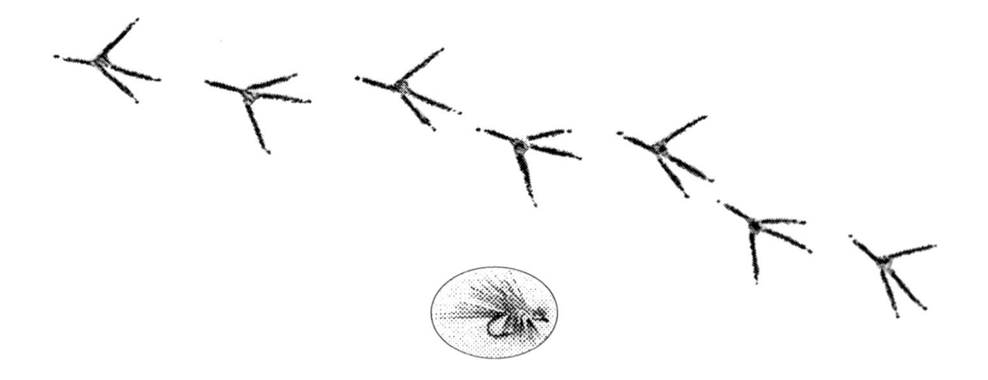

The Royal Guilt Fly

You'll never find it in your fly-tying manual, but believe me it works like a charm! As a matter of fact, the Royal Guilt Fly is an absolute one-of-a-kind, never-since-duplicated original. It always hooks 'em quick and deep, never lets 'em go! I should know because I'm the one who first designed and fished the Royal Guilt Fly with such extraordinary success.

I can't believe I'm actually giving this secret away after all these years, but it just doesn't seem fair to take such a sure-fire pattern to the grave with me, so I suggest you listen up.

By the time you're eight years old, and you've already been your father's only "son" and favorite fishing buddy for five long years, you have an expectation. That's why I had no place to put Dad's shocking dinnertime announcement: He'd be leaving before dawn the next morning with three *other* fishing buddies—and he wasn't taking *me!*

I slumped low in my chair for a moment, drowning in disbelief. Then I planned my perfect revenge.

Now, the achievement of any worthy goal always requires a significant personal sacrifice. In this case it would cost me one entire eyebrow and half of my girlish bangs, cut cleanly to the roots. Lay this fistful of hair across a #4 long-shanked hook, lash it all together with a tight figure-eight of thin-split Johnson & Johnson adhesive tape, slather the broad-winged quarter-pounder with enough Crisco to make floatation a remote possibility—and voila! You've got yourself a *real* Royal Guilt Fly...well, almost.

I nearly forgot to mention the importance of proper presentation. As with every piscatorial endeavor, finesse is everything. You must wait until your quarry finishes his breakfast, packs up his lunch...

> You must wait till a porchful of gear's piled tall,
> till the last duffle bag bumps down the hall,
> till those long-dreaded headlights dance on your wall—
> then you cast your best cast
> with no mercy at all!

"Bye, Daddy," I whisper sweetly from my bedroom shadows. He is frozen in mid-step, tasting the bitter betrayal he's about to dispense, caught like a slithering worm. I hold out a suitably trembling hand, manage to squeeze a hot tear from my eye.

"Here Daddy...(snuff-snuff)...I...*made* something...(snuff)...for you," I whimper pathetically, dropping the *Guilt* into his hand. "I hope you have...(snuff snuff)...a really f-f-fun time."

I finish with a mournful sigh, throwing my arms around his neck. The guy doesn't have a chance!

Now, that powerful Royal Guilt Fly became the proverbial gift that kept on giving. I can guarantee Dad never left me behind again. As an unexpected bonus, that innocent little fly delivered me from six weeks of outdoor chores lest neighbors surmise that this poor, pitiful, (obviously neglected and overworked) hairless child had somehow contracted a raging case of the mange. I make no apologies for any of this, even half a century hence; I still believe a girl's gotta do what a girl's gotta do, and if all is fair in love and war, I'm quite certain this includes fishing.

As for the original Royal Guilt Fly, it worked splendidly for more than forty years before meeting its final demise. When Dad passed away in 1995, our whole family gathered for a very special ceremony. One by one we told our favorite stories about my father, then each of us placed a personal treasure into a sacred bundle which rested over Dad's heart the day of his cremation.

I guess you know what my treasure was. That day the tears were real.

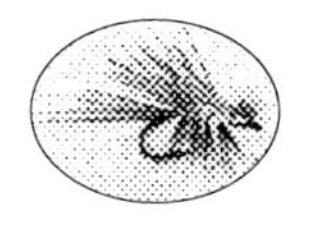

Heaven

There's a lot of folks who'll tell you God lives in the sky, but I swear, more than once I've found God at the far end of a fly rod. Why is this so darned hard to fathom? With a world as crazy as this one to manage, isn't *She* entitled to a few days off, too?

The Deli Special

It happens sometimes, you know—gals out-fishing guys. But only under a blue moon on the seventh Wednesday of any month that begins with R. It happens. And when it does, there's usually a stiff price to pay.

They'd already had their fun with me at the Brothers Cafe. I'd driven right by that place a hundred times, but I'd never eaten there before, unlike most of them, so I was ripe for the picking.

"The short-stack's kinda skimpy, T—so go ahead, order the full meal deal."

Right. It took both waiters and the cook to carry out the platter of hotcakes, which I could barely see over once they plopped it down in front of me.

Five guys were whoopin' and hollerin' and slappin' backs over that one. It *was* pretty funny, I'll have to admit, and I was laughing, too. That's the way it was with this gang of crazy fun-loving characters—Fast Eddie, Oxman, Harry, Dean, Steve, and me. Everybody took turns being the butt of the joke. Today was obviously my day.

Of course, I couldn't let them have the last laugh, so everyone was forced to wait while I soaked up about a gallon of Aunt Jemima and cleaned-up my plate. Just because I'm skinny doesn't mean I can't eat.

I was stuffed to the gills (no pun intended) and in considerable distress by the time we finally wedged ourselves back in the van, but I never let on. Where would be the victory in that?

We still had about another half-hour drive before we reached Chickahominy Reservoir, a truly ugly, odd-shaped hole smack dab in the middle of nowhere. It really does resemble the backside of the moon in this section of barren, high desert country between Bend and Burns. A few scrubby clumps of snaky sagebrush, a couple of broken down outhouses, miles of rocks and dust as far as the eye can see. Nothing pretty about it—except the fish.

These are unusually big, meaty rainbows, and there's plenty of them. They cruise the deeper portions of the lake, often running clear up into the shallow fingers until their broad backs are sticking halfway out of the water. Must be something they like hatching in the mud, but I'm no entomologist. I just know they're there sometimes—and when they are, that's where I like to be.

And that's exactly where we were on this day, six of us spread out along both sides of one of those shallow little arms, dredging for bruisers. We made a habit of starting out with a variety of flies to shorten the daily learning curve, but we all had our favorites; Carey Special, Prince, sizes 10-14; small Pheasant-tail nymph; black or green Wooly Bugger, sizes 8-10. On occasion a Stovepipe could work, and if you really got into trouble, maybe a big green leech would produce. Whatever the fly, Chickahominy isn't a fishery that surrenders its own without a good dose of patience.

It's a curious little place, and you can pretty much count on the wind. I've been blown off a rock by a water-spout I didn't see coming. I've seen bright stars in the middle of the day when a heavily-weighted fly was blown into the back of my head. I've hidden in the stinky outhouse when a game warden showed up and I'd forgotten my license at home. I've fished Chick' on breathless hundred-degree days and on windy winter eves when you couldn't make three casts before you had to chip the ice out of your guides. Downright miserable place sometimes, and we just kept coming back.

I'd gotten lucky right off today, hooking into the first fish, the second, and the third. Fast Eddie was fishing about twenty yards up to my right, casting flies and by now a fair number of sideways glances. He doesn't cotton to being skunked. Now others started getting into a few fish, too, but Eddie still hadn't touched one, and this was beginning to take its toll—especially when I just couldn't stop hauling them in, and the other guys couldn't stop razzing Ed about being out-fished by a *girl.* I figured I must have gotten lucky by casting over a little underwater spring. What else could explain the hot-streak I was having?

Eddie was a pretty good sport for a while, dishing out his own clever comebacks, but then it got kind of quiet. When I looked around for Fast Eddie, he was nowhere in sight. Eventually one of the other fellas passed by and told me Eddie was up under one of the nearby creosote bushes taking a nap. *Nap*, my eye. The old fart was pouting and I knew it.

"C'mon, Eddie, I know you're not sleepin'," I chided. "Come on down and I'll give you my spot." Most fellas would have been too proud to take me up on such charity, but not Eddie. He busted out of those bushes like a bull moose in the rut, nearly running me down as he hustled toward the water.

He started laying out his perfect, smooth casts, smack on the money, of course, because he'd been carefully studying the coordinates all morning. I moved up the shoreline a short ways, into the water Eddie had earlier abandoned. I made my first cast there, expecting to hear Ed's singing reel any minute now.

Yowser! It was a singing reel, all right—my own! One-two-three-*four* more fish in just as many casts. Eddie, on the other hand, working the magic spot even more furiously now, remained fishless. This is how I know God is a woman—a woman with one hell of a sense of humor!

Four voices immediately broke into a merciless litany of emasculating jibes that no man with an ounce of testosterone could have withstood. "Maybe you need to put on a nice little pair of lacy panties, Ed—maybe that would help?"

There was no end to the degradation. And I just couldn't stop catching fish!

By this time, a little gallery had collected, a few waders like us and a couple of other guys in a boat cruising slowly up the channel. Eddie motioned them in and moseyed on down toward their boat like he'd just met up with some long-lost cousins. The three were soon locked in an intense conversation, with Eddie occasionally pointing my way. Then they'd bunch up in a tight little huddle again. This went on for a good twenty minutes or so before the two suddenly jumped back in their boat and motored away.

Eddie is a trickster to end all tricksters. He'd taken his licks that day, and now he needed to get in a few of his own. As if divinely sent, these two sacrificial lambs had appeared precisely on cue. Oh, he'd worked those boatmen over in a way only Fast Eddie could—and it took them a full nineteen minutes to realize they'd been had.

I knew this because Eddie was half skipping up the beach now with a devilish twinkle in his eye. He always got like this whenever he pulled a good one—setting his chin and wallowing his dentures around in his mouth behind a most captivating grin. He'd never say right off what he'd done, but we knew it was coming, and the anticipation always had us giggling long before the story was told. Today was no exception. He was setting us up, waiting patiently for all five to gather 'round.

"Well, you know those fellas in the boat down there," he began. "They saw T catching all those fish, and they just couldn't stand it. Wanted to know what she was usin'." He flashed one of those denture-wobbling grins, released a dry chuckle to heighten the suspense. "I told 'em, you mean you don't recognize that gal? She's a good friend of Curt Gowdy's, you know. Why, she's on his fishing show all the time." He had them soundly hooked with that one. They wanted to know all about me and then, of course, Ed was more than happy to oblige. Before he was through with them, I ranked right up there with Amelia Earhart and Cleopatra, and they were *unduly* impressed. Well, he figured he'd strung them out about as far as he could, so when they got around to the inevitable question he went in for the kill.

"So what kind of fly did you say she was using?" they asked.

"Oh, it's a little somethin' we worked up together, kind of a custom design," he hedged. Now they were becoming his very best buddies, looked eager enough to pay cold hard cash if he'd just spill his little secret. "Well, you seem like pretty good guys—can you keep it to yourself?"

Yeah, yeah, they said. They'd swear on a stack of *Gray's Sporting Journals*, sell their grandmother for a hot tip like this.

They leaned in close as Eddie's voice softened. "We call it the Deli Special," he whispered, waiting just the right number of seconds.

"What's it look like?" they pressed. "How do you tie it?"

He had them staring into the palm of his hand as he began to paint the subtle details of this most mysterious fish-flogger. "Well sir, it's an easy fly to tie. You get yourself a #8 long-shanked *barbless* hook, see, and a *big* hunk of worm. Sandwich that worm between two little green marshmallows, then you just shove the whole thing right up—"

That's probably where the two lambs stopped listening and we all started howling. But I'm not sure—I only remember the tears running down my face.

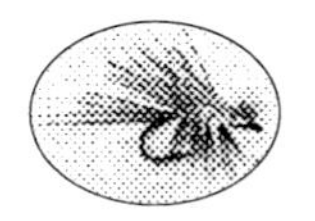

The River Church

This is my sanctuary,
the church God built for me Himself,
my secret haven where telephones
and endless obligations cannot reach me,
the place where I become like
two ends of a circle finally meeting,
the place where I'm most at home.

Guadalupe-River-Bottom-Pudding-Pie

Decadence on The Blitzen

What has five luscious layers, stands five inches tall (until it topples over), guarantees an instant bellyache, and makes you drive five hundred miles to get it? Guadalupe-River-Bottom-Pudding-Pie! And you get it by heading straight for southeast Oregon's Steens Mountain and the Donner und Blitzen River flowing from it. This provides a perfectly credible excuse for dropping by the quaint Frenchglen Hotel for dinner and an *awesome* dessert after a hard day of trout-chasing.

Now, pudding-pie was just one of many perks connected to this journey, and not the *reel* reason we always came back. It was a long-standing, late summer tradition for Dean Williams and his far-flung flock of cronies to converge here from all over the Northwest for their annual, four-day Blitzen Expedition.

I'd gotten thrown into the mix somewhere along the way and always looked forward to memorable days punctuated by fine dining, great fishing, and considerable streamside mischief. This year would be no exception, aside from the severe drought conditions that translated into unusually low water levels and extraordinarily high rattlesnake counts. *Everybody* was thirsty.

Now, I'm okay with snakes as long as I know they're around, but I don't appreciate many diamondback surprises. Fortunately, I was traveling with a half-dozen chivalrous serpent slayers who considered it an annual rite-of-arrival to clear the entire Page Springs Campground of any venomous visitors before yours truly stepped from her van. This custom had been firmly established the first year I showed up, when a triple batch of fresh-baked chocolate chip cookies instantly became the universally accepted bribe. (Come to think of it, sugar did have a strange power over this bunch.)

Our opening campfire always resurrected favorite stories from previous years, gave us a chance to s-t-r-e-t-c-h the lunker tales another inch or two

The Frenchglen Hotel, home of Guadalupe-River-Bottom-Pudding-Pie

with every telling. We laughed about how high Steve jumped that time we left the dead rattler coiled just outside his tent flap, and how quickly Jim "recoiled" after inadvertently *watering* the wrong, rattling sagebrush. Of course, there was always the debate whether this might be the year Dean finally crouched low enough to actually stick his nose in the river when stalking another one of his "really tough fish." In a few hours, all this good-natured ribbing would yield to a brand new chapter in the ever-unfolding adventure.

The rising sun threw a kaleidoscope of color across broad, steep canyon walls as I inched my way upriver. Tap-tap-tap. I moved like a blind woman through dry, rustling grass, my trusty wading staff sweeping and probing every rock, every bush along the narrow dusty trail in front of me. Cookies only bought me "in camp" snake protection—here I was on my own.

I'd been promised rattlers wouldn't pose much problem early in the day, but by afternoon they'd be moving down out of the hot rocky cliffs toward the cooler shade and shelter of the river—that's when I'd really need to start paying attention. Maybe so. Unfortunately, my snake scanner only had two settings: ON and HIGH, and it fired-up automatically at dawn.

After the first couple of uneventful miles, I began to relax, and when I crossed the mouth of Fish Creek, a passel of rising fry caught my attention. These were bright, lively little 6-9 inch rainbows. In the past along this stretch, we'd caught plenty of fish three times this size, but I've never been much of a trophy hunter. In my book, the thrill of hooking up with an ounce of anything native to a place more than makes up for sheer tonnage.

Small caddis were on briefly, and my little barbless elk-hair imitator did fine. When the hatch died, I spent some time discovering that a #16 Adams would also do, though surface action remained spotty far into the afternoon. Once dries get this small, I'm forced to use a "parachute" version—the little white tuft is the only thing that gives these eyes half a chance.

While I kept the guppies occupied with a lightly weighted Prince or Hare's Ear, my buddy Dean was working the water above the confluence with the Little Blitzen. He'd already landed one twenty-inch hog on a big black Woolly Bugger, and was now stalking another lunker even farther upstream. At least this was the newsflash offered by Gary as he hustled back toward camp for more gear.

Just a few minutes later I received a second bulletin—a swimming rattlesnake had drifted right by one of our guys as he waded in thigh-high water. Apparently, the snakes liked to hang out in the cool, dark undercuts, and swimming was one of their methods for getting there. Yowser! I'd been wading next to these same banks all day long, feeling plenty safe as long as I remained in the river. Staying puncture-free might be a bit trickier than I thought. Of course, none of these reports could be verified until hours later at dinner (if then), the slippery ethics of typical fisher folks being what we all know they are.

As the breathless day heated up well into the 90s, I continued to fish and move steadily upriver. Without a breeze, the canyon became an efficient solar oven, and standing in the cool water offered our only relief. I finally took a break for a late lunch in the lacey shade of a scraggly juniper. A few bites of my pitifully dry peanut butter sandwich didn't help much. Neither did the swig of lukewarm water that tasted like the plastic jug it came from. Man, I thought, what I wouldn't give for an ice cold mountain of Guadalupe-pudding-pie right about now. I started to salivate just thinking about it. Then my brain burped. Maybe it wasn't even on tonight's hotel menu. Oh, God! It had been a whole year—maybe they didn't even make it anymore!

Such obsessive concerns eventually drifted off into the Blitzen. I sat there a long time, mesmerized by the distant screech of hawks, the desolate poetry of this high desert canyon, lost in reverent wonder at what it must take for a tree, or a fish, or even a snake to survive in such a sparse and demanding environment.

It wasn't until the air suddenly cooled and deep shadows chiseled the rosy-golden face of the cliffs that I finally came back into myself. Trout were rising all around me now, but that didn't seem to matter. Dean and the others would soon be casting their way back toward camp, each carrying his own sweetly biased version of this day's tribulations and triumphs.

Within an hour or two we'd drift toward the long harvest tables of the Frenchglen Hotel dining room to lie and laugh, to guzzle wine and gorge ourselves on succulent home-style fare.

Once there, we bellied up to the table with folks we'd never met before—a dozen other hotel guests, many here for their first time, all quickly welcomed into our big jovial family.

After too much good food and more than adequate libations (because that's the Blitzen tradition), we abandoned all remaining reason to whoop

The Blitzen at sunrise

and cheer as the waitress climbed on a chair to announce tonight's eagerly anticipated pièce de résistance. Yes! Guadalupe-River-Bottom-Pudding-Pie—our favorite five-layer slide into decadent oblivion.

"And for those of you who aren't familiar with our world-famous dessert," she shouted above our raucous applause, "it's a rich butter pecan crust, filled with thick gooey layers of cheesecake, dark chocolate pudding, vanilla custard, and whipped cream. You really *must* try it."

And, of course, we did. Even fishermen can be polite.

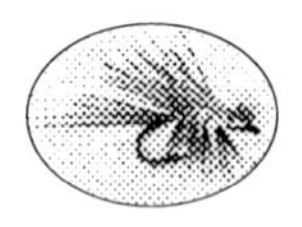

Worming My Way

Like many a devoted fly caster, my fishing career began with a worm in my hand. But in the slow, sure hatching of *this* fly fisherman, I had my own particular style of worming my way to the bug.

When I was a kid, a fishing trip started a good twenty four hours before you jumped in the car. If you really wanted to go fishing, it was your unspoken responsibility to over-water the back lawn all afternoon so night-crawler hunting would be profitable. Of course, your room had to be as spotless as the supper dishes before you were ever handed the empty Folgers coffee can and sent out into the starry night. In a Scandinavian family, you *work,* even for your pleasure.

Waiting was always the hard part. There was simply no point in going out before the sky went obsidian black, before the cricket choir was in full swing and wary earthworms had finally ventured forth, stretching plump pink, glistening bodies across the soggy ground—fishing fruit, ripe for the plucking. We moved like weightless ghosts on those magical summer eves, cool wet grass sliding between our bare toes, twitching fingers pinched in a perpetual "V" ready to nab the next slithering trophy.

Even the ensuing tug-of-war was a preparatory exercise in streamside finesse and patience. Any respectable robin knows there's no honor in ripping a worthy opponent in half. Stalking worms taught focus and mastery, too. All the while, the soft, golden beams of flickering flashlights swept eerily back and forth through the darkness. We always got our worm.

There's a favorite family story about the time my maternal grandfather received a rather harsh lesson in handling a granddaughter's budding piscatorial precocity. I was around four at the time, far too young to remember the details myself, but any chuckling relative was more than delighted to supply the necessary color.

My grandparents lived several hundred miles to the north in Tacoma, Washington. They didn't get to see me much, which meant each visit was a rare and welcome treat. I was, after all, their very first grandchild, so there was always considerable hugging, and kissing, and cheek-pinching whenever the occasion allowed. I *do* remember this because, even though I loved my grandparents dearly, those endless smooches were sometimes wet and actually kind of yucky. A good tomboy just naturally recoils from such disgusting things.

Teryl drowning worms on the McKenzie

During one late springtime visit, my father and grandfather decided to take me fishing on the McKenzie River, just a few miles and minutes from our home in Eugene, Oregon. As usual, I wasn't permitted to leave until my doting grandmother dressed me up like a (stupid) doll in another one of those (stupid) lacey, starched white pinafores she was so fond of sewing for me. This was, I much later understood, her not-so-subtle crusade to convert the heathen toddler into a lady.

Unfortunately, this faux-feminine subterfuge would fool no one but my most genteel and unsuspecting grandfather, nearly leading to his early demise.

Once we reached the river, I apparently wasted no time smearing enough dirt across my dress to get comfortable, and we began assembling our gear. Obviously, Dad hadn't bothered to inform my grandfather that I was already a self-sufficient and accomplished fisherman. With the best of intentions, I'm sure, Grandparent (as I called him) gently slipped the fishing pole from my hands and set to work threading a juicy night crawler onto my treble hook. Dad says the look of disbelief on my face was utterly priceless, but nothing compared to what followed.

As Grandparent handed the baited pole to me, I shoved it back with disgust. "Here!" I said. "If you're gonna bait the hook, you can do the fishing, too!"

Petite and curly-headed, dressed all in frills, I probably shouldn't have blamed Grandparent for assuming I needed his help—but God knows I *did* blame him.

Dad busted up on the spot, and it took my startled grandfather quite a while to recover. Rumor has it I pouted dramatically against a fallen log for several hours, refusing to fish or eat, most indignantly rejecting several heartfelt apologies before finally giving in.

Hell knows no fury like the wrath of a ticked-off granddaughter! Grandparent always kept his helping hands to himself after that—as a matter of self-defense.

Well, worms gave way to lures as soon as I was old enough to manage a spinning outfit. Dad set me up with a junior-sized fiberglass spinning rod, a nice reel, net, and my very own tackle box filled with all the necessary paraphernalia, times ten. I'd cast and retrieve for hours on end, running up to the cabin only occasionally to show off the latest "big one." It didn't take my parents long to figure out they'd invested in the perfect babysitter—always available (just add water), child-approved, and works for almost nothing.

A huge old ponderosa windfall stretched across the shoreline just below our Crescent Lake family cabin. The bottom twenty feet or so of this tree stuck out obliquely into the lake, its gnarly half-submerged root-ball providing perfect fish cover in about five feet of crystal-clear water. Many a day I'd nestle myself in the twisting embrace of those sun-bleached roots like some sprightly forest elf, trusty tackle box wedged to one side, peanut butter sandwich squashed in the opposite pocket, both hands fully occupied with the serious business of fishing.

Though I'd grown enormously fond of spin-casting, here it was always best to bait fish with worms or eggs, because on any calm morning before the wind came up, you could see right down into the water. Truth be known, sometimes I chummed a little—dropped in a worm, maybe tossed out a couple of bright orange salmon eggs, watched them drift slowly down through the tangle of roots, catch a subtle current, float off or settle peacefully into the olive green goo between the rocks.

It was always exciting to see who'd notice it first. Often as not, my offering wouldn't make it all the way to the bottom before some little rainbow or maybe a fair-sized kokanee darted from the shadows, snatched the tasty morsel, and sped triumphantly away. Sometimes brick-colored crawdads vied for the prize, scrambling from stone fortresses, dueling mercilessly with wee pincers slashing while pumping tails propelled them backwards through billowing clouds of green silt. A brand new adventure every moment. A bunch better than Nintendo!

Dropping a line in the water here was a lot like shooting fish in a barrel. If I held very still for a while, moving nothing but my eyes, the fish soon forgot I was there and resumed doing what fish do best—eat. From this keen vantage point, I could easily watch the entire drama unfold and know exactly when (or if) to set the hook. I wasn't after small fry, but occasionally a big bully wandered in to commandeer the pool, and I wasn't above teaching it a lesson.

If the fish weren't biting or I got terribly bored, I might unscrew the white enamel lid on that cute little jar of fish eggs and pop one into my own mouth. Hmmm. A bit too salty to eat more than a couple at a time. I never tried the worms.

Now, I didn't always fish by myself, though generally this was the case. Some days Dad wrapped up his cabin construction projects early and invited me to join him for an evening of slow trolling around the lake. Catching our limit of kokanee became less and less of a thrill toward the end of every summer, so on one of these much-too-predictable evenings I decided to try something new. Instead of gearing up with the usual cumbersome string of gaudy flashers with a red and white Spin 'n Glow trailing behind, I went *pure*—just the monofilament line with nothing but a tiny brass swivel attached to a lonely fluorescent lure. Just for giggles, I draped a snake-sized nightcrawler around the lure's treble hook and plunked the whole darned mess over the side before my father took exception.

"What the heck are you doin'?" he growled, figuring I should know better.

"Just tryin' something," I mumbled.

Dad stared blankly into the water for a moment. "That *thing*," he said, "has no action at all."

Of course, he was right, but I wasn't about to admit it. The big wad of worm had taken all the wobble out of the lure, that was for sure. Even at trolling speed, it just sunk like a stone.

Dad saw the set of my chin and knew what it meant. "Fine," he muttered. "Have it your way." Then he settled into an uneasy silence.

Sure enough, he kept landing fish after fish while I just sat there trolling a stone. An hour passed, maybe two. I was way off somewhere when my rod jerked *hard,* twice, then bent and held so steady it was obviously snagged on the bottom. Dad saw what was happening and instinctively cut the engine so we wouldn't lose the gear.

Suddenly the bottom *moved.* Line started stripping from my reel, the tension set light for the soft-mouthed, average-sized kokanee. But this was no kokanee! I looked to Dad for reassurance, but he had none to give. The man who usually had all the answers was as dumbfounded as I was, but neither of us had time to ponder.

As small as I was, I had to stand and lean back, or it felt like whatever I'd hooked would have pulled me straight overboard. Dad reeled up his own line as fast as he could, doing his best not to foul mine, which by this time was zig-zagging wildly back and forth beneath the boat.

"Keep the tip up!" he shouted. But that was mighty hard to do.

We both kept fumbling with my reel tension until it finally felt right, loose enough not to pop the line but tight enough to put some reasonable pressure on *whatever* eats stones.

Twenty yards of line screamed off the spool. I cranked in a dozen, yielded five, pumped in ten, lost a dozen more. Forty-five minutes into the struggle, a sizeable cluster of other boats had gathered around. Davida (the female version) and Goliath were locked in mortal combat. It took every ounce of my strength and focus to keep that rod tip up.

By this time my proud papa was grinning like a Cheshire cat, and I heard a voice way off in the distance shout something about a Mackinaw.

"Yep, she lands this fish and we'll get her on the Andy Maxon Show," Dad yelled back, referring to the local TV fishing show.

I remember thinking, Wow, won't that be something—the Andy Maxon Show. Man, I wanted this fish! My skinny little arms were throbbing, weighed a thousand pounds each, but I wasn't giving up.

It was getting dark when we saw the first flash. We only saw it for a second, and this is going to sound strange, but the first thing my brain said was "sea turtle." It was *that* big, and at age ten I lacked any other meaningful reference. But my fantasy was short-lived.

The huge fish dove once more, but with far less conviction. I reeled in line with relatively little resistance, and Dad reached for the puny little trout net, never meant for anything this size, but it was all we had.

The fish rolled slowly one last time, crossing under the boat and forcing me to lean over the bow to keep up with it. Dad followed me quickly to the starboard side.

"We're only going to get one shot at this," he warned.

He was on one knee behind me, bracing himself and reaching the net far into the water. I worked the fish slowly back toward him, reeling in line, raising the rod tip almost to vertical, trying to bring the monster alongside. The angle was bad but it was now or never. Dad made his move.

With one smooth sweep he captured only half of the big trout in the net, lifting it toward the waterline in what was now a valiant two-armed attempt to flip the heavy, struggling fish over the gunwale and into the boat. It became one of those surreal, slow-motion movies then—a freeze-frame explosion of water, the blurred arc of my father's flexed arms, the net, the huge dark fish passing before my eyes, a windshield, a dull thud, an instant of grace, a gasp, a splash, an unbearable silence.

We did not speak for several minutes—we cried. Over and over my father apologized. "I'm sorry, Teryl…I'm so sorry."

The enormous Mackinaw (lake trout) had simply been too large for the net. When it struck the top rim of the boat's narrow windshield it had teetered a moment, fallen the wrong way onto the bow, slid over the edge, and returned to the watery depths. At some point, the fatigued monofilament had snapped, and a great fish eluded the Andy Maxon Show.

It is the way of the world sometimes. And it hurts.

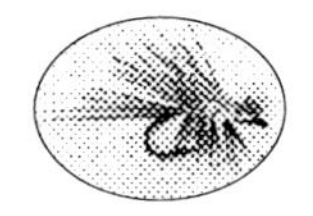

OFF SEASON
Oh! I'm badly hooked by you,
Dear Trout — far beyond your watery lair,
my thoughts, my hands, my heart cry out
to winter's Sweet Despair!

THE MAGIC CADDIS

Fat-wrapped, gold-bodied, Bucktail Caddis #12-14—my all-time favorite fly. The reason for this stems way back to a hot August day on central Oregon's Metolius River, where one particularly bedraggled little caddis fly just wouldn't quit.

I can hardly keep a straight face thinking about it now. I'd been told over and over again, "The shape, the color, the size, everything has to be just right." Maybe so for the fisherman. Apparently nobody told the fish.

A blistering summer sun was finally sinking mercifully behind the thick curtain of giant ponderosas as I finished working one of my secret pockets along the upper stretches of the river. Actually, the Metolius is more of a stream here because it originates not far above, emerging from a prolific network of icy springs released beneath the shadow of Black Butte, a massive ancient cinder cone. As cold and clear as any water you'll ever wade (and survive), the burbling rivulet soon accepts contributions from Lake Creek and other minor tributaries, quickly becoming more than impressive.

A ways downriver, swirling eddies and deep channels surrender to racing azure flats, then suddenly drop away into bottomless pools where monstrous

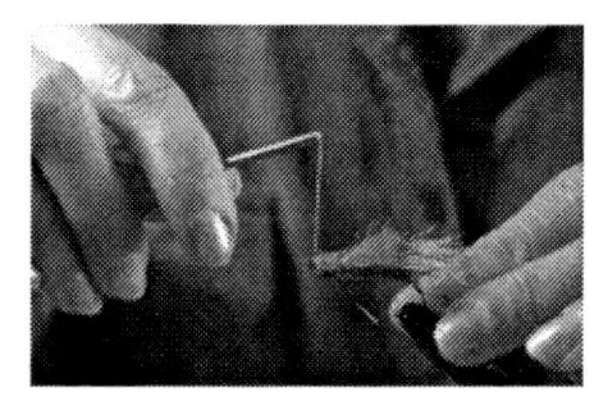
The author tying a fly

bull trout lurk, easily holding smaller cousins at bay. This is the locally-famous *Dolly Hole* known for producing an occasional thirty-incher. (Bull trout are often mistaken for Dolly Vardens, but the Dolly has never inhabited the Metolius. "Dolly Hole," however, still *sounds* much better than "Bull Hole.")

The Dolly Hole is located adjacent to the aging Wizard Falls Hatchery, which once provided all the upstarts for making this highly pressured river as productive as it is. (Note: The Metolius stocking program ended in 1996; the wild, catch-and-release-only fishery is making a remarkable comeback, and hatchery descendants are now virtually extinct.)

Most of the Metolius looks like picture-perfect magazine water, but it's tricky. Without knowing its temperament, a fisherman can waste an entire day working ideal spots where nothing but your imagination swims. It's best to learn this river from a veteran like I did—my sympathetic mentor, Fast Eddie. He shared some of his secrets, left the rest up to me.

When I reached the Dolly Hole, the late afternoon caddis hatch was on, and my little golden standby was certainly doing the trick. I've seen good fishing before, but this was insane.

I worked the close water first, as I'd been so stringently instructed to do. That's as far as I had to go. One, two, three short lazy casts yielded as many feisty, deep-bellied beauties—one wild rainbow and two less colorful, fin-clipped planters, all running 12-14 inches. I checked the barbless caddis, quickly dried and regreased it. It was doing all right.

Must admit I was a little startled when the next few casts brought similarly instant results. All planters this time, but who cares? With water this cold, wild or otherwise, no fish is a slouch.

It was almost too easy, close to unfair. I thought about moving but asked myself why? After the fifth or sixth fish, my fly began to show some expected distress. The razor-sharp teeth were taking a similar toll on my thumb, now oozing a wee bit of red into the water whenever I grabbed the next unhappy jaw, gently rolling out the hook.

I make it a practice rarely to net or actually land a fish, preferring instead to release them quickly while still underwater. Eddie taught me to slide one hand down the line, maintaining tension while the other wet hand grasps the gaping lower jaw. This way I can usually back out the barbless hook without even using a hemostat, freeing the fish with minimal harm.

"Too many folks think just because a fish swims away, it's gonna live," Eddie said. "No, sir." Lots of fish die within a day or two of being caught, he explained, victims of ignorant and unintentional, but still deadly, mishandling.

"You touch those gills," Eddie said, "let a dry hand mar their slimy protective coating, that fish is a goner, just a matter of time."

Eddie wasn't interested in turning me into a fish-killer. There wasn't a day when his firm riparian ethics didn't echo in my ear.

Well, I sharpened the hook once and lost count at eleven or twelve fish. I almost retired that amazing little fly when the thread wrapping the body finally popped and began to unwind. What the heck, I'd give it one more try. Replacement was nearly imperative once the ratty hackle feather finally let go, and the golden yarn body went the way of the thread, but by now it was getting downright entertaining.

I never saw a more pathetic excuse for matching the hatch. How many "naturals" still fly with ninety percent of their wings chewed off, sporting a now hairless metallic body and trailing not one but two extra-long mutated tails—one of frayed yarn, another, the pitiful remnants of what was once a leg-faking hackle feather? This baby had style!

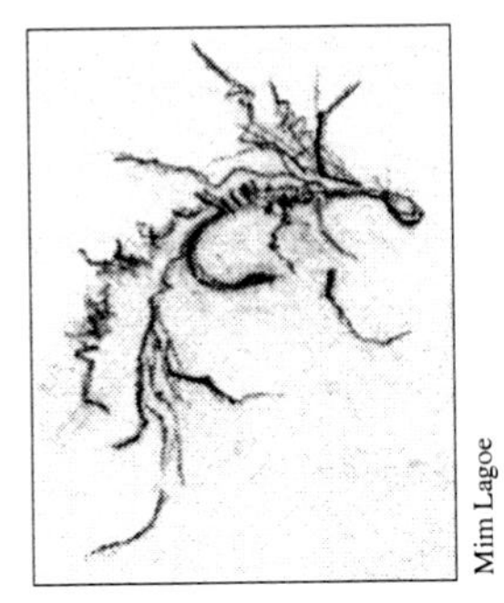
Mim Lagoe

The magic caddis

That darned fly was pure magic, nobody can argue. It happens sometimes and we never know why. Is it really the fly itself, or do we enter some kind of altered state when it works just because we *know* it will? I suppose there's really no answer. The river gods just bless us once in a while. It's best not to pry.

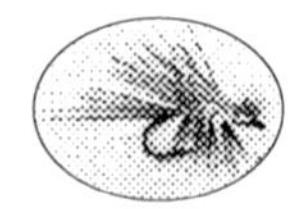

Redside Rodeo

Pteronarcys californica—with a name like that, I'm surprised they hadn't been run off at the Oregon border. Maybe someone tried, but they sure hadn't succeeded because I kept hearing about this crazy salmonfly hatch that hits the Deschutes River every spring, somewhere between May 15th and June 10th. This mystical event always seems to be accompanied by days of incoherent babbling:

"You ain't gonna believe it!"

"Oh, you shoulda been there Wednesday—fish as big as battleships!"

"Too bad, you just missed it! Maybe next year."

What sets it off, rumor claims, is water temperatures finally breaking fifty degrees. Then the first big black bugs crawl out of the river at the lower end, and over the next several weeks their upstream cousins gradually get triggered. So do hourly water samples and binocular sightings, endless wagers and pontificating, and urgent midnight phone calls reporting the inch-by-inch progress of the hatch. It's enough to turn civilized fly casters into glassy-eyed, slack-jawed nut cases. And most of these are my friends.

Salmonfly

"This is the year," they kept promising me. "We're gonna haul your scrawny little fanny down to Dry Creek so you can just see it for yourself."

After listening to years of effusive hype and knowing such things rarely live up to expectation, I quietly prepared myself for yet another stellar disappointment. But when the car door flew open, so did my mouth—and in crawled about a half-dozen of what they'd been talking about.

You'd have to multiply every adjective by ten before any description could begin to match the surreal phenomena now swarming in front of my eyes. Every reed, every branch on every bush along that entire riverbank was squirming with fist-sized gobs of two-inch, black and orange salmonflies. Lower branches were so heavily laden they dragged in the water where the broad, slurping mouths of trout greedily plucked them clean. Thousands of split nymph skeletons littered the rocks, and the air was thick with miniature, fluttering Kamikazes careening, colliding, and crashing as leaping fish snatched manna from the sky. The surface of the river danced as though a giant hailstorm was stalled permanently overhead. I'd never seen such urgent and animated frenzy.

Frenzy is contagious—we suddenly became as rude as these legions of salmonflies, scrambling over each other and grabbing madly for our gear. Eddie tossed me a bright orange #6 Sofa Pillow, which would be hacked to death in a matter of minutes. I was already false casting half-way between the car and the river, itching to join the fray. Guess who was the glassy-eyed, slack-jawed nut case now!

The huge, clumsy naturals tangled in my hair, banged off my sunglasses, crawled up my nostrils and my sleeves, but I didn't care. They dropped from the sky like sputtering helicopters, hit the water like bricks. This was not a day for casting finesse or delicacy; this was a day for just smackin' it home.

The *big* fish knew where the smorgasbord was, and they were all bellying up to the table at our feet. By the size of some of those snouts, the broad flashes and powerful swirls, we knew we were dealing with the real gunboats here.

With so many naturals on the water, competition was stiff, but it didn't take long to figure out that the harder the fly smacked the water, the more it got noticed and the better it worked. We were ridin' and ropin' at the Redside Rodeo National Championships—YeeeeHAAAW, we just let 'er buck!

I lost count at twenty-five fish—twenty-five mature, meaty rainbow "redsides," many of them ranging 15-22 inches, the usually elusive bruisers feeding with reckless abandon *right up on top!* My 9-foot, 4X leader shortened itself to a 6-foot, 3X in a heartbeat, costing me a handful of very nice flies. But it also shortened my learning curve; in rare conditions like these, a dust-bunny hooked to an arm-length of piano wire would likely suffice.

Well, we followed that astounding hatch for several long days, moving as it moved, until we and it finally burned out. A week later, a couple of us die-hards tied up a bunch of fresh #4-6 Sofa Pillows and Rogue Stones, and returned to see if any of those gorgeous redsides still remembered the feast. A few smaller ones did. But the bushes were all bare by then—only a handful of late-comers sputtered through the afternoon air, and few fish rose to the occasion.

It was actually pretty quiet and sad. Kind of like going back to the fairgrounds a few hours after the cowboys leave town. The bucking chutes are empty, the crowds have all gone.

But if you sit alone in the grandstands a while and listen real close, you can still hear that cornball announcer bellowing in your ear—*"Great show, great show! Same time, same place next year. Now all you buckaroos and buckarettes—Y'all come back, ya' hear!"*

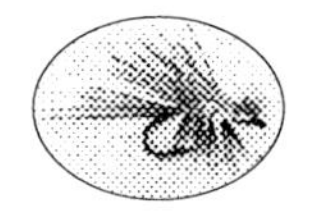

Professor Brown

Don't you just love it when someone swears "There's no fish here!"—and then you catch one right under his nose? This has to be one of life's most delightful, unexpected gifts, and I unwrapped a real doozey on one of those sublime central Oregon summer days while studying the secrets of the mighty little Metolius River.

My good buddy, Mike Oxman, knew the river well and had kindly agreed to take me on a reconnaissance mission. It was a scorching day; it even smelled hot. The late afternoon air was filled with the raucous squawking of jays and chattering squirrels when we parked our car in the welcome shade of a giant ponderosa located about midway along the most fishable section of the river. It was well short of the point where the Metolius dives sharply into a deep gorge, and pitons might be a wise addition to a fly box.

Not far away stood a small bridge we planned to use. The Metolius takes a lot of pressure all season long no matter where you fish it, but we counted on fewer people fishing the other side.

As we headed upstream along a dusty footpath worn through the tall grass, Mike explained how tricky this little river could be—how so much of it looks like textbook fishing water, yet how few of these spots actually hold fish.

I'd certainly experienced the truth of this fact on several humbling occasions, which is precisely why I was so grateful to finally be in the company of an expert. (An *expert* in fishing, I soon discovered, is anyone who guesses right about twenty percent of the time.)

A few hundred yards upriver, a deep cut-bank caught my eye. "How about that place?" I pointed with my rod.

"Nope," Mike said. "Nothin' there."

I believed him for an instant—then the hunch hit. We took a few more steps before I dropped back. "Gotta try that spot," I explained.

T and Fast Eddie fishing the Metolius River

Mike answered with a wry grin that said, "Fine if you want to waste your time." Then he continued upriver until he was almost out of sight behind a thick screen of willows.

I tied on a #12 Renegade, resorting to a little trick I'd picked up in Montana: Fish it out dry, bring it back wet. Double coverage. Worth a try.

I was fishing a beautiful 9-foot custom 6-weight rod built especially for me just a few months before by one of my Montana chums. He'd even inscribed my name on it—*Ms.T*—to give it the magic touch. That rod made me look like a much better caster, so I loved it dearly.

Crouching several yards back from the edge, I made a couple of lobbing casts in close, let the powerful current pull the fly down and around. Nothing. Maybe Mike was right.

Might as well check out the rest of this water while I'm here, I figured. A few yards at a time the casts lengthened until they were falling just short of the opposite bank. The water runs swift and deep here, but still clear enough to see bottom in most places.

It was a ridiculous amount of line to put out in a spot like this—it bellied out in a heartbeat, and no amount of mending could keep the fly dry. The Renegade had plenty of time to sink deep before even the quickest retrieve brought it back under the ledge beneath my feet. That's really what I was after, anyway—a dredging operation of sorts, something that would drag the fly through the dark shadows of that undercut, way down deep where the lunkers might be.

Damn. Snagged. I worked it and jerked it upstream then down, trying every angle to break free. I wasn't in the mood to lose another fly, and I sure as heck wasn't keen on advertising this predicament to my buddy after ignoring his advice.

Looked like there wasn't much else I could do now but eat a little crow. I reeled up and lowered the rod tip into the water, applying enough direct pressure to pop the 4x tippet. But instead of popping free, the fly line started to move. Not much. Just a few inches. I thought I felt a heavy, slow tug as though I was hooked to the proverbial rubber boot. Then the "boot" trembled once and sunk a smidge deeper. My heart pounded like a drum. Mike loves to tell this part of the story:

"All I hear is this little far away voice hollering, 'Mike! *Mike!*' I look down to where T is and see her rod bent almost double, and she's frantically waving me in with her other arm like she's trying to get a search plane to land."

He dropped everything and came a runnin', big grin on his face when he saw the pickle I was in. It was a fish, all right, and a good one, too. But try as I might, I just couldn't get that doggone trout to budge from under the bank. Mike knew I was still pretty green at handling a fly rod because he'd been the one to convert me to fly fishing just a year or so before.

We were laughing now—this whole thing was a *big* surprise for both of us. Obviously, I was fresh out of ideas for what to do next and finally ready to accept some suggestions.

"Give me your rod a minute, T—let's see what I can do." Mike's more than a foot taller than I am and could extend the rod higher and farther out over the river, creating a much better angle to invite the trout out of hiding. After ninety seconds or so of steady pressure, he finally coaxed the trout into the body of the stream.

At this point, Mike obviously forgot our "give me your rod a minute" agreement and began playing *my* fish! I reached for my rod a couple of times, but he brushed me off like a pesky mosquito. I finally slugged him in the arm to bring him to his senses. Once he snapped to, he had the dazed, startled look of a kid caught with his hand in the cookie jar.

"Call dial-a-prayer if you want some sympathy, Bud—gimme my *#@$ rod!"

Chances are I didn't play *our* fish nearly as artfully as Mike might have, because I let that rascal dart right back under the bank. Thank God it tired more quickly this time, soon returning to open water. This seemed like a good thing for a split second, until I watched that crazy trout suddenly shoot some fifteen feet upstream into a broad, deep pocket of calmer water.

As if it had practiced this evasive maneuver a hundred times before, it instantly and most *intentionally* wrapped the tippet *twice* around the broken branch of a submerged log. There it rested peacefully at the slack end of a short tether. And there I was again in a no-win situation.

By this time Mike was guffawing, well aware he'd never get hold of my rod again and equally aware I had no clue what to do next. To this day he claims he's never seen a more pitiful hangdog look on anyone's face. It was enough to elicit one last sage piece of advice.

"Try taking the pressure off the line, Miss T."

I did as he said, and watched in disbelief as that Ph.D brown trout methodically unwrapped itself from the branch and dove straight back under the cut-bank. All I can say is anyone who claims a fish can't think never met Professor Brown.

I did eventually land this astonishing fish, without doubt the most beautiful brown trout I've ever seen—deep bellied, tail as broad as my hand, spots so big and bright somebody could have painted them on with a felt-tip pen. Brown trout of any size are quite rare in the Metolius, which is largely dominated by rainbows—plenty of hatchery graduates (in those days) and a few nice natives.

Mike guessed this brown at more than seventeen inches and three pounds. Scrappy and smart, a real trophy by any measure—and it belonged right back in the river.

Professor Brown more than earned his right to confound yet another unsuspecting angler on another glorious Metolius day, so it was with great pleasure that we both watched him swim away. This magnificent specimen had smartly outwitted us on several counts—by being there in the first place, by being a brown trout and a large one to boot, and by being so incredibly feisty and clever.

An experience like this really makes you stop to think. That's what a good professor does—makes you think.

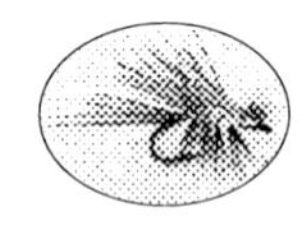

The Bear Essentials

Dismay is too gentle a word. Terror, a bit too harsh. Perhaps there is no word for describing one's emotional state when discovering your vast fishing arsenal still lacks one absolutely essential item—a 12-gauge shotgun!

Dear God, what had I gotten myself into? Warm water fishing buddies had told more than enough spine-tingling tales about carrying a loaded pistol in your float-tube "so you can get those sneaky water moccasins before they get you." I wasn't going there.

Ah, but I'd dropped my guard when the husband of a dear Alaskan friend invited me to witness the annual arrival of the salmon—the "kings" (Chinook) and "reds" (sockeye)—as they made their famed spring runs up the Kenai, some heading for the high reaches of the Russian River. That's where we'd be waiting for these great silver monsters to jerk our arms out of the sockets. Sounded like a good time to me.

Part I
Russian Roulette

It's never easy getting an energetic family of four headed in the same direction. By mid-morning my generous hosts, Barb and Ed Neumann, had stowed our supplies, hooked-up the tent-trailer, and managed to herd both kids into the back seat of the car at the same time. Like most men, Ed aimed to travel from "Point A to Point B, ASAP," but thankfully my buddy Barb was there to lever her husband into the scenic tour for this greenhorn Oregonian.

We made our first obligatory stop at Portage Glacier, a groaning, crackling expanse of frozen barrenness about fifty miles southeast of Anchorage. A broad, glassy lake stretched from where we stood to the distant pale blue ice cliffs, gifting a perfect reflection to double an already breathtaking view. Right then and there, I fell passionately in love with Alaska. No camera could ever hold enough film to capture my awe.

The twinkle in Ed's eye said plenty as I casually inquired (again) about the likelihood of encountering a streamside grizzly once we reached our destination. "Don't you worry now, T," he said, "I gotcha covered."

I suppose his light-hearted reassurance was intended to ease my mind. It didn't. All I could think about was the anemic advice written in some Girl Scout manual a hundred years before: "Make lots of noise, clap, sing, ring bells, play dead if you're ever attacked." This and an old joke that didn't seem so funny anymore—about how you can always tell when you've stumbled across genuine bear scat because of all the shiny little bells in it!

After a gorgeous but lengthy drive, made even longer by nervous anticipation, we finally reached our campsite, settling in for the night. I stalled as long as I could during breakfast the following morning, but the moment of truth finally came. Ed grabbed his fly rod, swung a well-worn rifle scabbard over his shoulder, bid a hasty farewell to the family, and motioned me into the woods.

I deserved a whopping ticket for following much too close as we threaded our way through the damp, thick tangle of brush and trees he called "the path" to the Russian River. In more familiar surroundings, these gentle sounds of wind and calling birds moving through the forest canopy would have lulled me into a deep state of relaxation, but here my head was swiveling a full 360 degrees with every hyper-alert step, doing whatever it could to ensure we had no bell-belching, four-legged company.

We walked on forever, it seemed, and I was emotionally exhausted by the time the sound of rushing water finally reached my ear. We hadn't seen a single bear the entire way. I'll always wonder how many saw us.

One quick scan up and down the vacant riverbank soon put my concerns to rest. Obviously, the salmon hadn't arrived yet, but I still wasn't disappointed.

The author releasing a Russian River rainbow

So this was The Russian River I'd heard so much about, not far from where it's swallowed by the mighty Kenai. When the run finally did come in, I was told, the whole mouth of the river would be clogged with shoulder-to-shoulder fishermen, both the two-legged and the four-legged kind. Today, we had the swift, emerald depths all to ourselves. Suited me just fine.

It was pushing noon before our boots touched water. Dead ahead was a nice looking flat, but nothing was rising, so we geared-up with a couple of different wet flies, searching for a winner. Both the soft-hackled emerger and the weighted #8 Hare's Ear instantly produced. I swear those fish would have hit a bobby pin—it didn't seem to matter what we used, we'd landed smack dab in the midst of *hungry* Dolly Varden heaven.

Now, these weren't big fish, at least by Alaskan standards, fourteen to nineteen inches tops, but plenty scrappy enough to keep us thoroughly entertained for the entire afternoon. Ed was fairly new at fly casting, looking for some coaching along the way. I managed to squeeze in a few pointers between non-stop hoots and hollers. As suspected, Ed was a natural and soon casting like a pro, so we split up before long, leapfrogging our way through each enticing pool and riffle as we moved methodically downstream. Here the Dollies surrendered to huge, hog-bellied rainbows, hugging the deep sweeping undercuts where free-drifting salmon eggs would soon pile up in this year's succulent feast. My cheeks nearly cracked from hours of grinning.

Yep, that cinched it; when I croak, I'm coming back as a pretty little 6-weight fly rod. Think of all the amazing days like this I'm gonna see! Unfortunately, this particular picture-perfect day ended much too soon as the light began to fade.

"Just a few more casts," I begged, but Ed's gentle patting of his gunstock was enough to underscore the sheer lunacy of retracing ten thousand steps back to camp in gathering darkness—a point I was quick to concede.

We spun tales for a circle of five that night, huddled tight around a crackling fire. There's something downright magical in the not-quite-blackness of a brief Alaskan summer night. It's written in the glowing faces of tall-tale-telling friends twirling marshmallows over neon coals, in the strange new comfort gained from a slug-loaded 12-gauge shotgun leaning handily against a nearby tree. It lingers like the haunting memory of a dear old friend whose name we can't quite remember. And it's never quite done with us.

Deep in our almost forgotten interior there waits an essential, primal longing for the occasional whiff of danger on the hot, raw breath of a country this wild, this unpredictable, this *free*. Again and again it asks the ever-present question that keeps us truly alive: What's lurking out there in the shadows, just beyond the ring of dancing firelight, and am I still wild enough to face it?

Give me one more chance at The Russian River, salmon or no. I'll pack my own shotgun next time—and gladly pay a ransom fit for "kings."

Part II
The Real Katmai Fishermen

It *is* definitely possible to have too much fun. I have proof.

Now, it isn't often I'd willingly opt for a day of watching someone else do the fishing, but on this particular morning, arms still aching from more than a week of non-stop red-wrestling, an opportunity to switch places for a few hours brought most welcome and wondrous relief.

I'd been hanging out with a few adventuresome chums in the heart of the Alaskan Peninsula, on the expansive shores of Lake Clark. With several float planes at our ready disposal, it was simply impossible to decline the pilot's generous invitation to fly us into Katmai National Park for a relaxing day of bear-watching.

Katmai is known for supporting the highest concentration of grizzlies anywhere in the world. My pulse quickened when I learned we'd be fishing, at least part of the time, in close proximity with these ferocious half-ton giants. We might even get a chance to hike into Brooks River Falls, a world class destination for professional wildlife photographers. Many spectacular calendar shots of salmon-swatting bears had originated at this very spot. Would we be lucky enough to encounter the real Katmai fishermen in action today?

I stepped most gratefully into the icy, ankle-deep water beneath our plane's beached pontoons, having clutched a paper bag close to my chest for most of the bumpy ride to the park. This typically overcast, mid-summer day still carried a hint of coolness on the breeze, one slow deep breath settling my queasy stomach as I escaped the gently bobbing fuselage. It was *so* good to be back on terra-firma or aqua-firma, it made no difference to me.

Sloshing toward shore, we were immediately met by several park rangers assigned to educate each arriving party. Nothing is left to chance in Katmai, lest poorly informed visitors soon wander into potentially disastrous circumstances without recognizing the genuine danger they're in. We were allowed to fish as long as we kept constant vigil and maintained a safe distance from the bears. If we landed a salmon, we were to proceed promptly to a

Sockeye salmon ("reds")

well-fortified fish-cleaning building, where we could safely prepare and store our catch. If a bear approached while we played a fish, we were instructed to quickly cut our lines and slowly back away. If a bear challenged us for a freshly caught fish, we were to drop it on the ground and retreat calmly without delay. Several days before, in the lobby of our fishing lodge, I'd taken a close-up look at the deadly, outstretched five-inch claws of a towering *stuffed* grizzly—there wasn't going to be an argument.

The river was swollen with spawning reds, their coppery hook-jawed snouts bumping my boots as I waded deeper for a cast. Might have saved myself the trouble, I suppose, just grabbing them up in my hands, but that hardly seemed fair. Besides, today wasn't really about fishing anyway, it was far more about just being here amidst all this incredible power and beauty, about being very small in the greater scheme of things, and knowing it full well.

More than a bit uneasy around my four-legged fishing companions, I took false comfort in the fact that I'm skinny and wouldn't even make a good snack. Like they say, you don't have to outrun the bear, you just have to outrun *one* of the people you're with. Heck, I figured with the right motivation I could easily set a new personal best.

So I fished, or pretended to fish, but mostly I took internal snapshots of this great, timeless drama unfolding all around me—this plethora of courageous, invincible beings returning to their origins against such terrifying odds; these massive, gorging predators celebrating their own survival amidst this astounding movable feast; the broad, mirrored flats reflecting it all while sliding silently, eternally, toward a faraway sea.

My trance was broken by a sharp whistle from somewhere behind me. I turned to see my comrades collecting excitedly around our tethered plane. They were peeling off waders, breaking down rods, and tossing duffle bags toward the cockpit. "Hurry up, T," someone shouted. "We're heading for the falls!"

A park ranger would lead us through the dense forest to Brooks River Falls, but not before carefully reviewing the rules. We were solemnly reminded about the extremely high population of grizzlies in this immediate area, the absolute necessity of observing every precaution: Stick close together. If one person stops, we all stop. Make plenty of noise. If a bear appears suddenly, remain calm. Surrender the trail, back away slowly. Make no sudden movements. Never turn your back. Never run.

We all registered the gravity in the ranger's voice. Each rule became a somber mantra as we followed our fearless leader, single file, into the trees. Our smaller group had merged with several others at the trailhead, so we were now about a dozen in all, trekking toward an extraordinary experience none of us could yet fully appreciate. We talked loudly, laughed nervously, clapped and whistled and sang. And believe me, we stayed very close together for the several mile hike to the falls.

We were approaching the river when our ranger suddenly dropped back to hurry us along. A sense of great urgency flooded the group as we were quickly ushered up a steep flight of stairs surrounded by high walls of heavy chain-link mesh. We spilled into a large, sturdily-built platform enclosure approximately 15 x 20 feet in size, perhaps 10–12 feet off the ground. A massive metal gate clanged shut behind us.

It took me a moment to process this utterly unexpected, completely foreign experience, for I was suddenly the animal in the cage inside this strange zoo in reverse, a zoo obviously created to protect the only species in immediate danger here, the fragile, gawking human. Meanwhile half a dozen bears of every size and description roamed freely around us. Clearly immune to our presence, they went on about their peak season business—fighting, fishing, and feasting.

We were not the first to enter the observation platform this day, nor were we the last. The far front corner was already crowded with some very professional-looking folks, and a most impressive array of microphones, tripods, and video cameras panning the remarkable scene below. An excited whisper shot through the crowd: "*Wild Kingdom* is filming a show!"

Our outrageous good fortune escalated, on cue, as another young ranger's running narrative about the intricate life cycle of these bears began to flow toward the microphone.

I was just learning that these unusually large inland brown bears and the more notorious grizzly bears are now considered to be the same species. More fascinating facts ensued when suddenly the speaker gasped in mid-sentence, "Oh, boy—this is going to get *interesting*!"

Quickly redirecting our focus with his outstretched finger, the young man gazed intently downstream. "Here comes Papa!" he exclaimed, "and it ain't gonna be nice."

Grizzly at Brooks River Falls

There, wading up the very center of this broad, raging river, came the most massive male grizzly my imagination could hold. The frothing white water buffeted high against his powerful chest, yet he moved as smoothly and effortlessly as a Mack truck crossing a mud puddle. I could almost feel the deep, rumbling throb of diesel engines as his great shoulders rolled and rippled with each steadily advancing stride. His dark, ominous gaze, fixed directly on the falls ahead, never wavered. Every trace of wildlife melted into the woods as he passed.

As if he'd directed this exact scene a thousand times before, the ranger called out each shot. "Watch the old sow now, down there on that big rock just below the falls," he announced. "That's the prime fishing spot. She'll back right off, but she hasn't seen him yet."

Sure enough, as the big male approached, the female sensed a threat. Glancing downstream, she tensed, turned sideways momentarily, lowered her head in submission. Then as delicately as any prima ballerina, she slid backwards into the swift current and quietly drifted away.

Two inattentive juveniles still frolicked just above the upper break of the falls, having missed this critical cue. "Those cubs are much too close," the ranger warned. "They'd better watch out!"

The next instant, a dripping brown monolith lifted up from the riverbed, dwarfing the huge, recently surrendered bolder now under his exclusive command. With one casual toss of the mammoth head, a great reverberating roar escaped his gaping jaws, and two very startled, very lucky youngsters evaporated into the trees.

Now the master went to work. Again and again, one swipe of the deadly paw knocked a leaping sockeye into the swirling eddy just behind the rock. The bear lunged into the river, each time emerging with yet another flopping salmon in his teeth. He half-walked, half-drifted to the shallows of a small, nearby island, where he nonchalantly bit off the top of the fish's skull and

The Real Katmai Fishermen

slashed open the pale belly to extract the glistening roe. Then he cast the bulk of the bloody remains onto the gravel. At times when fish are this plentiful, gourmet feasting rules the day.

Lesser bears eventually wandered back into the river to fish, but none was ever foolish enough to challenge the broad, invisible boundary clearly established by this dominant bear. Imagine our horror, then, when one of the *Wild Kingdom* cameramen suddenly emerged from the dense foliage beneath our viewing platform and began wading out across the shallow back-channel, apparently hoping to plant a remote microphone somewhere on the carnage-strewn island. One casual glance from our giant protagonist, and the cameraman had a rapid change of heart (and underwear, I'll wager). I've never seen a man walk on water before—a truly impressive sight.

Impressive was everywhere I looked—in the rugged beauty of the rambling Alaskan landscape, in the wondrous, wild creatures inhabiting it, especially these magnificent Katmai fishing bears.

But nothing, *nothing*, matches the impressive determination of a salmon heading home. Endless numbers have made their courageous journeys up countless rivers for thousands and thousands of years.

We were given the rare privilege of being here for just a few hours, on one particular river, on one particular day in eternity, to silently cheer them on.

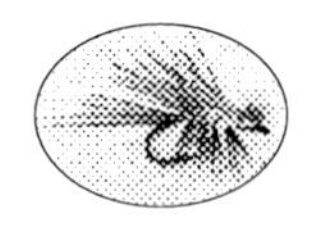

Teryl "T" Johansson with
flyfishing mentor "Fast Eddie" Suttner

It Takes A River

Sometimes, it takes a river
to unwrap the odd gift
of a human life,
yet ribbon by ribbon
by river's sliding silver rift,
the precious package comes untied.

In the soft fog
of an endless becoming,
some find it hard to know when
the slippery path is finally underfoot,
except in watery reflection.

Beneath the shadow of a sky-bound pine,
one easily forgets—*all* grandeur springs
from a tenacious tangle of tiny roots
far beneath the surface of things—
only when a river swallows half of me
can I, at last, remember…

There are many ways to find our face
and learn our truest name,
but the purest, surest way perhaps
is to stand alone in fluid silence.

How much has been retrieved
on wisp of feather riding breeze,
settled still on morning glass!

How many breathless hours
bequeathed to rising trout,
but keen excuse for wading farther out
toward shadowy realms
in search of *me!*

If ever I knew a soulful friend
it surely was the wily brown
who pulled me deep and held me there
long enough to finally drown
all I am *supposed to be...*

Oh, sacred gift of primal gill and fin,
loan me just one borrowed hour
to swim beyond these mortal shores,
set a weary spirit free!

God knows it takes a river.

About the Author

A native Oregonian, Teryl "T" Johansson likely waded before she walked—by the age of three she had already become her father's only "son" and favorite fishing buddy. Teryl has fished the West for half a century now, many of those years with a fly rod. One of her solo fishing trips lasted four months and covered nine western states—9,000 miles of blue-ribbon trout water. She's not your ordinary gal.

Tim Hall

Teryl "T" Johansson

"When I have a rod in my hand," she says, "I'm not a man or a woman—I'm a being with a need, and a means to fill it."

With profound respect for the sacredness of a fishing life, "T" credits much of who she is to quiet, contemplative time on the lakes, rivers, and streams of her childhood. "The wilderness has always been my church," she explains. "That's where everything makes sense."

An avid fly fisher and accomplished freelance writer, Johansson's articles have appeared in outdoor magazines such as *The Flyfisher*, *Salmon Trout Steelheader*, *Cascades East*, *Trout*, and *Flyfishing*. She lives near the Wallowa Mountains of northeastern Oregon, where she continues to write and to worship the Divine with her fly rod.

Established in 1999, Bear Creek Press of Wallowa, Oregon, specializes in publishing books unique to the Pacific Northwest, especially those that capture the life or preserve the history of the region.

For more information or a free catalog:

Bear Creek Press

814 Couch Avenue • Wallowa, Oregon 97885

541-886-9020 • bearcreekpress@eoni.com

www.bearcreekpress.com

Bear Creek Press gives one-day service on all orders and an unconditional guarantee on every book.